JUNGLE ATTACK

"You—sonsofbitches!" I grated out, trying to focus, going for the Star .45 automatic in the holster under my jacket. I just got the gun out and was aiming it at the brawny man's chest, when the big, hard shoe of the tall man cracked hard into my wrist, sending the stubby automatic pistol flying across the room.

I yelled again in pain, and began struggling to one knee awkwardly. But the pipe came again then, connecting this time in a glancing blow across the side of my head. Bright carnival lights flashed on inside my skull, and I was suddenly riding a wildly careening rollercoaster, falling down the steep track and jerking around corners violently. And all through that there was a loud ringing in my ears, like an alarm going off. The rollercoaster car jammed to a jerking stop, though, and I had been kicked in the stomach as I lay on my side on the floor.

That kick took the rest of the fight out of me, and all I could do was lie there and gasp for air, trying to suck lungfuls of it in, feeling like I was going to retch. Through that I was kicked three more times. The first one caught me under my ribs, in my side, and felt like it ruptured something. The next one punched hard into my back, cracking at the bone of ribs and spine. Finally, the last one crunched against the back of my head and put the carnival lights out for good, sending me giddily downward into a black and seemingly eternal abyss.

Other books in the SOLDIER OF FORTUNE series:

- #1: **MASSACRE AT UMTALI**
- #2: **THE DEADLIEST GAME**
- #3: **SPOILS OF WAR**
- #4: **THE GUNS OF PALEMBANG**
- #5: **FIRST BLOOD**
- #6: **AMBUSH AT DERATI WELLS**
- #7: **OPERATION HONG KONG**

We will send you a free catalog on request. Any titles not in your local bookstore can be purchased by mail. Send the price of the book plus 50¢ shipping charge to Tower Books, P.O. Box 511, Murray Hill Station, New York, N.Y. 10156-0511.

Titles currently in print are available for industrial and sales promotion at reduced rates. Address inquiries to Tower Publications, Inc., Two Park Avenue, New York, N.Y. 10016, Attention: Premium Sales Department.

Soldier of Fortune #8:

BODY COUNT

Peter McCurtin

TOWER BOOKS   NEW YORK CITY

A TOWER BOOK

Published by

Tower Publications, Inc.
Two Park Avenue
New York, N.Y. 10016

Copyright ©MCMLXXVII by Tower Publications, Inc.

All rights reserved
Printed in the United States

BODY COUNT

ONE

The river boat squatted heavily at dockside, bulky and obese on the night water, a dull yellow light probing weakly through the slatted windows of its cabin. It smelled malodorously of rancid engine oil and bilge water, and fingers of rust marred its wide-beam hull, streaking a faded and flaking white paint. Sitting there moored to the wharf by thick hemp ropes, the old hulk bore a close resemblance to the fat sewer bug that inched its way cautiously up the nearest rope to the gunwale.

I stood staring at the *Papuan Princess* somberly, beginning to think that maybe I must be a little crazy, or at least a bit feeble-minded, to even consider heading upriver into the depths of the New Guinea jungle in that tub. But I had sold the rifles to Ruyker, after all—the weapons he was so wantonly arming the Kiwais with—and I had not been able to refuse a plea by the authorities in Port Moresby to find Ruyker and try to buy the guns back from him before he caused a native bloodbath of spectacular proportions.

To understand the gravity of the situation, you had to know both Ruyker and the Kiwai tribe. Ruyker was one of the toughest, hardest men I had ever met, and that was before he had gone psycho and started selling modern weapons to stone-age hut-dwellers. Over the ten years or so he had buried himself in the forests of New Guinea, trading with the primitive men there, he had hardened even more, apparently, to the point at which something human had gone out of him. There was something primeval inside him now, something very uncivilized—maybe subhuman.

I had had no way of knowing that, when I sold him the German Volkssturm VK-98 rifles in Sydney, and had not asked him what he planned to do with them. Later, when I learned from Australian authorities that Ruyker was re-selling the guns to a completely amoral society of aborigines who would use them against their neighbors as a kind of sport, I reluctantly felt an obligation to help them abort Ruyker's abhorrent project.

I squinted toward the boat now, as a dark figure detached itself from the cabin and hailed me. "Is that you, Rainey? Come on aboard!"

It was Averill Connors, the Australian army major in charge of the small detachment of troops there at Kikori, on the south coast. I was sure he had never guessed he might end up in a hellhole like that when he put on his country's uniform back in Canberra, but somebody had to do that service. I walked up the small gangplank and met Connors just as I stepped onto the deck of the *Papuan Princess*.

"This is it?" I asked balefully, hoping that Burke Ardrey owned some means of transportation other than this heap of junk metal.

Connors grinned. He was a squarish, slightly bowlegged fellow with premature gray hair and very dark brown, translucent eyes. His complexion was beet-ruddy from the sun, with a spattering of dark freckles across a rather thick nose. He wore khaki shorts and tunic and held one of those wide-brimmed Aussie hats in his left hand.

"Not to worry, old chap. It's serviceable, you can wager on that. Wait till you see Ardrey. He's as bloody crusty as the boat. Come on into the cabin, he's anxious to meet you."

I followed Connors to the cabin past piles of rickety crates stuffed with rotting tropical fruit and other, unidentifiable cargo, and ducked as I passed through the low cabin hatchway. Inside it was slightly more spacious than I had imagined, and had a cleaner look than out on deck, but it was littered with papers and liquor bottles. Burke Ardrey rose from a chair at a small table in the center of the cabin, and extended a grizzled, tanned hand to me.

"Well! Jim Rainey! You don't look nearly so bleeding sinister as the major here painted you. My pleasure, my boy."

I took Ardrey's hand. He was a rugged-looking character, with a three-day growth of beard and deep bags under his eyes. He was not a big man, and he was past his prime, but he had a wiry, physical look about him.

"Glad to meet you, Ardrey," I told him. "I hope Connors hasn't been telling tales about me."

"None of it," Connors said. "I just said you'd be a good chap to have along on the *Princess* if Ardrey should run into trouble this trip."

"I'm glad you're going, Rainey," Ardrey grinned roguishly. "Sit down, lad, and I'll pour you a glass of the smoothest brandy in the East."

We sat around the small table, which had a

wrinkled map spread out on it. "I'll pass up the brandy," I said. "I figure I'd better stay sober over the next week or so, if I'm going to find Ruyker."

Undeterred, Ardrey poured himself and Connors a shot of liquor, explaining how it was good for his constitution and protected him from backcountry bacteria. Connors winked at me, enjoying himself. We had hit it off pretty well from the beginning, Connors and I. He had been wired from Port Moresby, telling him to help me to get transportation into the interior, and to offer protection if I wanted it. I had declined taking one or more of his men with me, though, because I wanted to keep a low profile with the natives, and I figured most of the danger was from disease-carrying insects, malaria, and other nice little unseen predators of the jungle. As it was to turn out, I was wrong.

Connors and Ardrey swigged their brandy, and Ardrey stuck a stubby finger on the old map. "Here's as far as the *Princess* goes," he told me. "We call it Bik Pella Post. You can't navigate the river up past that. If Hendrik Ruyker is dealing with the Kiwais, you'll have to go north from Bik Pella, into the hills. You ever been in there?"

I shook my head negatively.

"Well, lad, you've got a bloody experience ahead of you," Ardrey grinned, showing a missing tooth at the corner of his mouth. "The fuzzy-wuzzies get pretty backward in there. They eat each other, you know. I mean, they have a regular feast from time to time. Usually it's somebody from an enemy tribe, but they're not all that particular. The Kiwais ring their villages with head trophy poles, and the Danis kill for sport. They play at war like Englishmen sit down to a good chess game."

"You make it sound pretty primitive," I admitted.

"Primitive?" Ardrey echoed, in his rather gravelly voice. A kerosene lamp over his head cast grotesque shadows over his face as he peered up at me from under heavy brows. "Primitive, you say? Heh! Primeval is the word, my lad. There are tribes in those mountains who have never seen a white man, and have no idea that they are surrounded by a mighty ocean—in fact, have no concept of what an ocean is. These are not men as you know men, Rainey. All they know is 'pointing the bone' and curing scalps and smearing their own feces over their naked skins."

"Well, nobody's perfect," I offered.

Connors grinned. "Ardrey just wants you to know what you're letting yourself in for. Even most of the old-time B-4's haven't been in Kiwai or Bamu country." B-4's, I knew, were long-time Aussie and British residents of New Guinea. "But, then, with Ardrey guiding you from the river, you ought to be all right."

Ardrey had agreed to go inland with me from Bik Pella Post, and take a couple of his *Princess* crew for porters. But he did not seem happy about going to look for Ruyker. He had had some bad dealings with Ruyker, in Kikori and Port Moresby, and harbored a deep dislike for Ruyker. He looked up from the map now, and stared into my face soberly.

"I'll get you where you want to go, lad. But what if we find Ruyker? How do you plan to talk him out of those rifles?"

I shrugged my shoulders. "With money. As much as he could make in profit by re-sale to the Kiwais."

"Why not just take them from the sonofabitch?" Ardrey asked pleasantly.

I smiled. I liked his style. I started to reply, but Connors did it for me.

"Because the government wants it all done peacefully," he told Ardrey.

Ardrey shook his grizzly head. "A bloody good deal for Ruyker, I'd say."

"If we get those rifles back, it should be a good thing for all of you here," I reminded Ardrey.

"That's it," Connors agreed. "The Kiwai chief, Kokoda has been terrorizing neighboring tribes since his first purchase of guns from Ruyker. He has almost wiped out his old enemies, the Bamus. Now he's threatening to rule central Papua on his own, with more weapons, and deny governmental authority at Port Moresby. If that happens, maybe the B-4's in Port Moresby and at the Cricket Club in Rabaul will quit reading newspaper accounts of the bloody back-country war, with their guesses at body counts and head trophies, and realize that Ruyker and Kokoda pose a threat to our continued survival in New Guinea."

A glum silence hung over the table, after that summary. I finally looked over at Ardrey. "I suppose you people make me pretty much as big a villain as Ruyker," I suggested to him. "You and your B-4's."

Ardrey held my gaze. "If we did, I wouldn't be taking you into the interior, Rainey. No, business is business. You can't be held responsible for what Ruyker is up to. The fact that you're going in there makes you A.O.K. with me, lad."

"Same here," Connors told me.

I sighed heavily. "Well, maybe I can help undo what Ruyker has begun. I really hope so. When can we leave?"

Ardrey began folding the map up. "Tomorrow I must load some bolts of cloth and some tools for sale in Bik Pella Post. Make it the following day, at dawn."

"I'll be here," I told him.

"And remember, the Kiwai tribe inhabits a fairly big territory. From what I hear," Ardrey told me, "Kokoda has given lesser chiefs the power to deal in his name. Ruyker could be almost anywhere in a very big area. There is also the rumor that he may start selling to smaller tribes, if he can't get bigger prices from Kokoda. So if you can narrow our area of search somehow, it would be very helpful."

I nodded. "I know. I still have a couple of people to talk to. Maybe they will have something." I rose, and Connors and Ardrey did, too. "I'll see you day after tomorrow, Ardrey. Bright and early."

"I'll be here," Ardrey grinned, showing the hole in his teeth.

Connors offered his help, the next day, in running down information on Ruyker. But Kikori was not a real headquarters of Ruyker, so he had no roots there. There were no employees to talk to, and he was a man without friends. He had an office of sorts in Port Moresby, down the coast, but a brief stop there, on my way to Kikori, had gotten me nothing. The one employee of Ruyker I had found there had been very close-mouthed, under orders, and would say only that Ruyker was operating out of Kikori for a while. Here in Kikori, I found that Ruyker had stayed at the Owens Guest House for about a week, and then had left for the interior less than a week ago, with several native porters who regularly accompanied him.

In the morning I tracked down a native who had worked for Ruyker a few months ago, a fellow who lived on the outskirts of town in the aboriginal shanty-town there. Kikori was just a small frontier-style town, with a few two- and three-story buildings centrally located and a few paved streets. Beyond that there were jungly side streets and dusty compounds and a stinking, rat-infested waterfront on the river mouth. The few white men who lived there by choice must, I figured, have a screw loose somewhere. At any rate, I found the native in his shack on the edge of town that morning—a dark, smelly place that held the sun's heat like a bake-oven—and he was sick with a fever and hardly recalled Ruyker's name. I got nothing from him. He had not seen Ruyker in almost a year, and knew nothing of his present activities.

But he gave me a lead. He mentioned, in passing, that whenever Ruyker was in town, he went to see Nellie Waki, a half-caste girl who was employed by a local saloon owner.

Just after lunch I went to visit Nellie. She had the afternoon off, it seemed, and I found her at her room in a three-story frame building that had been made over from a commission merchant's warehouse to a rooming house. She was on the top floor, in a suffocating little room. She met me at the door with a tentative smile.

"Yes?" she said in English, when she saw that I was Caucasian.

"You're Nellie Waki?" I asked her.

She nodded. She was quite a pretty girl, actually, despite her aborigine blood. She had kept the sensual aspect of the primitive, and sloughed off the crude, in the mating of white blood with native. She had a rather finely-chiseled face, except that the nose was too broad. The high cheekbones added something to her beauty, as did the rather sensual mouth and eyes. She kept her tightly-curled hair short and rather close to her head, and it was dark brown rather than the usual black. Her skin was light coffee-hued, and very smooth. She wore a rather short one-piece dress that revealed a good figure, and she was barefoot.

"Yes, I am Nellie," she replied.

"I wanted to talk with you about Hendrik Ruyker," I told her.

She narrowed her eyes slightly, and then smiled a knowing smile. "Ah! You are friend of Hendrik. I understand. You come in, please."

I did not know what she understood, but I went on into the hot room, and Nellie closed the door behind me. The place was spartan in the extreme, with only a bed in a far corner, and a small table with two crude chairs to my right. A hot plate stood on a box on another wall, and I gathered she must use toilet facilities outside the room, down the corridor. There was no dirt or litter around, and no odors that were unpleasant to the nostrils. She went immediately to a window and jammed it open further, and then turned and smiled at me.

"It is okay, you are Hendrik's friend." I thought the smile was a formal one, though. "He has sent them before. You take clothes off, we make sweet-talk-nice-touch, okay?"

Before I could respond to that, Nellie was suddenly pulling the dress off over her head. My jaw dropped slightly as the garment came off and dropped to the floor. Nellie had absolutely nothing on under it. Her cafe-au-lait skin shone in the soft sunlight from the window, making highlights on her perky breasts and flaring hips and long, firm thighs.

"You like Nellie?" she asked modestly. "You maybe want kissy-kiss in nice place, yes? I do for you. What is your name, mister?"

I managed to close my mouth finally. I started to tell her that I had come to conduct a very different kind of business from this, that I wanted to question her about important matters. But then she came over to me and slid her arms around my middle and touched her mouth to mine, probing tentatively with a small, pink tongue. My hands had found her curves of their own volition, and suddenly I no longer cared all that much about talking about Ruyker. She was so seemingly eager for my body that it was all a little overwhelming. I wondered absently how she could create intimacy with such abandon and then hope for any kind of payment for it later. The impression she gave was that she was irresistibly drawn to masculinity, like a moth to flame. If it was an act, it was the best one I had ever encountered, and I have been in some of the best brothels in the world.

While the kissing was still in progress she was fumbling with my clothing, and then suddenly was giving a healthy massage to a very vital area. To hell with Hendrik Ruyker, I thought as she slowly turned my groin into the center of the universe. That could come later, the interrogation. I had had a hard few days, and was entitled to a brief respite offered so graciously. The girl looked clean, and she did not give herself to just anybody, or Ruyker would have had nothing to do with her. With a few deft unbuttonings and unbucklings, my clothes, too, hit the floor, and we were magically on the narrow bed at the wall.

I have had a couple of women, and some of them performed what they did best with what could only be called a wild enthusiasm, but Nellie knew things I had never encountered before, and she loved doing them. She did things with the tongue that still make my groin ache to think about. Much sooner than I wanted to be, I was past ready, and we were joined in a hot union, with Nellie making strange, stone-age sounds in her lovely throat, and hugging me tightly with bronze, sculptured knees, and moving those flared hips with such expertise that no motion was lost, no friction of smooth-working parts missed in the heat of the moment. In the center of all of that there was a sharp gasping, a ragged, throaty noise, and it had come from the depths of my chest as we climaxed in a sweaty, trembling ecstasy of twisted bedclothing, entwined limbs, and damp flesh.

I could not leave her immediately. The thought did not even occur to me for several minutes after it was all over. Something deep inside me, something perhaps as primordial as the thing just under the surface of Nellie's perfect body, had accepted the fact that I had just experienced a kind of finality, and that nothing could happen now that was not anti-climax.

Later, as we lay touching all along the length of our bodies on the small bed, I was more relaxed than I had been since my arrival in New Guinea, and it occurred to me that maybe that dark island of jungle and fever was not quite all a green hell, after all. When I asked about Ruyker, finally, she talked freely about him.

"Oh, yes. I see him this time here."

I lay on my back, staring at the ceiling, with a Cuban cigar stuck into my mouth. I would much rather have stayed in that room over the next several days, than head out into a bush country that had not changed at all for five thousand years. "I understand he went to see Motu Kokoda again—the big chief of the Kiwais."

"He say Kokoda's name very too much, yes."

"Did he mention any other places he might be going?" I asked, not caring a whole hell of a lot.

She thought a moment. "He want glitter-rock from Bamu, too, he never have all too-much, I think."

That was what Ruyker primarily traded for the guns—the gold ore that the natives picked up in the mountain streams. At one time, there had been a gold rush at Port Moresby that rivalled the intensity, if not the numbers of prospectors, of the Sutter's Mill insanity of 1848 and '49.

"Ruyker intends to sell guns to rivals of the Kiwais?" I asked Nellie now.

She looked over at me. "Guns? I do not know these."

That was all she gave me, but it was enough. It meant, if it was true, that Ruyker was even crazier than I had thought. To give guns to another tribe besides the Kiwais might build up his weapons business, but it would create sheer havoc in the jungle area where he sold them, and also would not make Kokoda very happy with Ruyker.

When I left Nellie's place that afternoon, in a rented Land Rover, another car followed me across town and then disappeared before I reached the dilapidated Goroka Hotel. I put it out of my mind as unimportant, and got in touch with Burke Ardrey, and he told me the information helped a lot. When we left the river at Bik Pella Post, we would make a trip into Bamu country first, which lay south of the Kiwai territory. Maybe we would get lucky and find Ruyker there. There were only a few Bamu villages left, since the recent Kiwai gun terror, and we would head for the big one, where the Bamu big chief—a fellow called Nanabe Merah—just might be trying to buy guns of his own from Ruyker.

I went out to a nearby greasy-spoon restaurant for a late dinner at nine, and returned to the hotel intent on hitting the sack early. I had a big day ahead of me the next morning. When I entered the run-down lobby of the hotel, though, I had a small surprise waiting for me. Two men were there to greet me—tough, hard-looking Aussies—and they had gotten rid of the desk clerk, so that we would be alone. They were both dressed in rather soiled tropical cotton suits, with bulges under the jackets.

"Are you Rainey?" the tallest of the twosome asked me, as I came across the lobby to the desk, to get my room key. They moved to station themselves between me and the desk.

"What if I am?" I said, looking them over. The

shorter, brawnier man bore a very thin scar across his mouth and chin, and had a broken nose.

"Nellie Waki says you're going after Ruyker," the brawny one said to me.

"That was while she was still able to talk," the tall one grinned harshly.

My face clouded over. "You hurt the girl?"

The brawny man shrugged. "She's a fuzzy-wuzzy, chappie. And she was a pain in the bloody ass. Just like you, only not so bloody bad."

I looked from his face to the long, bony one of his taller companion. "Who the hell are you?" I asked them.

The tall one grunted out a brittle laugh. "We're friends of Ruyker. We want you to leave him alone, old sport."

"I didn't know Ruyker had any friends," I countered.

"Well, let's call us business associates," the brawny man amended their claim.

My eyes narrowed down, and I got the message. "You're suppliers of Ruyker?"

"Our employer in Port Moresby is," the tall one said.

"Shut up," the brawny one told him.

"You're going to sell him more guns, aren't you?" I guessed.

The brawny one moved closer to me. "The word is out that you're going to interfere with Ruyker's trading in the interior. Particularly you're going to try to stop the selling of guns."

"Only a maniac would sell rifles to those primitives," I said evenly to him. "All I'm going to do is reason with him—maybe buy the rest of his rifles back that I sold him, if he still has any."

The tall man shook his head. "Wrong, Yank," he told me. "You're going to get on your bleeding white horse and ride out of this little fairy tale. There's a freighter leaving for Port Moresby tomorrow, and you're going to be on it."

I gave them both a hard look. "Go to hell," I said in a low growl. I started on past them.

Somehow a pipe suddenly grew in the fist of the brawny man, and the tall one slipped on an old-fashioned set of real brass knuckles. I did not see the pipe come at my head in time to avoid its brutal swing entirely, and it connected with my neck and shoulder, the brawny man grunting with the effort as it connected. I gasped loudly as rockets of raw pain shot up and down my back and neck, and then I was hitting the floor on my side, blood running from the base of my skull.

"You—sonsofbitches!" I grated out, trying to focus, going for the Star .45 automatic in the holster under my jacket. I just got the gun out and was aiming it at the brawny man's chest, when the big, hard shoe of the tall man cracked hard into my wrist, sending the stubby automatic pistol flying across the room.

I yelled again in pain, and began struggling to one knee awkwardly. But the pipe came again then, connecting this time in a glancing blow across the side of my head. Bright carnival lights flashed on inside my skull, and I was suddenly riding a wildly careening roller-coaster, falling down the steep track and jerking around corners violently. And all through that there was a loud ringing in my ears, like an alarm going off. The roller-coaster car jammed to a jerking stop, though, and I had been kicked in the stomach as I lay on my side on the floor.

That kick took the rest of the fight out of me, and all I could do was lie there and gasp for air, trying to suck lungfuls of it in, feeling like I was going to retch. Through that I was kicked three more times. The first one caught me under my ribs, in my side, and felt like it ruptured something. The next one punched hard into my back, cracking at the bone of ribs and spine. Finally, the last one crunched against the back of my head and put the carnival lights out for good, sending me giddily downward into a black and seemingly eternal abyss.

TWO

It will never be clear to me exactly how I got out of my bed where the hotel management put me, on the following morning at dawn, and limped down to that river boat. But I arrived there shortly after dawn, with Ardrey waiting for me. The thugs had not visited him, apparently thinking that there was no reason to intimidate him too. They had done a job on me.

When I limped aboard in the gray light of a new day, Ardrey just stared hard at me for a couple of minutes, looking as if someone had just delivered some incredible news to him.

"What in the bloody hell happened to you, lad?"

I leaned against the gunwale of the *Papuan Princess* and tried to keep my head from floating off my shoulders. I was dizzy and nauseous, just from walking down to the waterfront from the hotel. I had a big hurt inside me, under the ribs, that I could only hope was not serious, and one posterior rib felt busted, but was probably just badly bruised. In addition to that, I hurt all over, and my face was all swollen and bruised.

"You look like a bloody van ran over you," Ardrey added.

"I got a visit from some business associates of Ruyker last night," I told him. Three or four flat-nosed, woolly-headed aborigines were stacking cargo crates on the deck near us—part of the crew of the *Princess*. "I don't think they like the idea of my going out to look for Ruyker."

Ardrey clucked his tongue. "That's the way it is, here at Kikori. Men do pretty much what they bloody well please. We'll report it to Connors, of course."

I shook my head. "To hell with that. Let's just head upriver, Ardrey. That's what I'm here for."

Ardrey studied me closely, then nodded his head. "All right, Rainey. They're your bruises. But I'd be willing to delay the departure until tomorrow morning, if you think you might feel more like leaving then."

"There's no time for delay," I told him. "Ruyker may be selling guns to the Bamus now."

"The Bamus?"

"That's right. Nellie Waki thinks he's heading for Bamu country. She mentioned Nanabe Merah."

Ardrey nodded solemnly. "Ruyker is really playing with fire, it seems. Well, at least we have a better idea of where to look for him. We'll head for Merah's territory after leaving Bik Pella Post. Maybe we'll catch up with Ruyker while he's trying to make a deal with Kokoda's arch-enemy."

"That's what I'm banking on," I told him.

The sun was just creating a low horizon of trees near the river when the *Papuan Princess* pulled away from the docks of Kikori and headed upriver, toward the interior. The slow chugging of the diesel engines seemed a comforting sound after the hectic night I had had. The native boys worked all around us, moving freight and piloting the rusty old fifty-foot tub out into the middle of the muddy river. As the morning brightened, I could see other boats all around us, plying the brown waters of the estuary. Most of the traffic was doing just what we were—trading with the villages of the interior. Most of the craft were smaller than the *Princess,* and some were only dug-out canoes. As bad as I felt that morning, I could not bring myself to go below and lie down on the lumpy bunk Ardrey had prepared for me. It was all new and interesting to me, despite the way I felt. All along the shoreline were strung tiny villages, as we left Kikori, until we got well upriver. As the morning wore on, Ardrey dropped anchor a couple of times, in midstream, and canoes and small boats came out from aborigine villages to trade with Ardrey. Then, as the villages thinned out to almost nothing, we began seeing wildlife along the banks—cockatoos chattering in the high, dense foliage, and crocodiles lying mud-caked on the hot banks. I knew that there were also, in that forest, green tree pythons, jungle fever, and deadly unseen maladies like the laughing death. It was not a habitable corner of the world, and I could only wonder at the kind of primitive man who did inhabit it.

In late morning I finally went below and rested, and I needed it more than I had imagined. Lying there listening to the thumping of the engines behind me, and knowing what kind of a world I was headed into, I wondered about the wisdom of my accepting this mission on the part of the Australian government. It was bad enough to have gun-toting thugs beating on you with skull-crushers and threatening you with sudden expiration. But I had the suspicion that what I had been through last night might seem like a Sunday picnic at the Cricket Grounds in Rabaul, if the head-hunters of the interior took a dislike to us.

Ardrey had had some contact with the really primitive tribes off the river, but not all that much. His business kept him on the river, where civilization had made its inroads into a stone-age world. Men wore bones in their noses, all right, and painted their faces in such a way that the sight would scare a grown man out of his wits, seeing one on a dark Kikori street at night. But the river people were tame by comparison to the tribes in the jungle. They had had to give up head-hunting and cannibalism in order to trade with government-licensed dealers like Ardrey, and they would never go back to that now. But only a day's walk inland there were men who had never seen the river and its mark of civilization. These were called "uncontrolled people" by those in official posts like Connors, and it was a descriptive phrase. It was hard for an outsider to comprehend the mentality of these savages, and there were true stories about them that made excellent grist for the Port Moresby cocktail hour. On my way through that town I had heard a story about a recent episode inland from there, in a much more civilized area than the one where Ardrey and I were going. A sick aborigine came to a river and was too weak to cross on his own, so asked help from two men from a neighboring tribe that was friendly to his. The two men, deciding the man was too heavy to carry across the river, bashed his skull in with a stone axe, rather than refuse him aid, which was considered inhospitable. That was the way some of these people's dark minds worked, and it was a way that would probably remain a mystery to civilized man for some time to come.

It was two days upriver to Bik Pella Post. The rest of that first day was spent largely on my bunk, but the second day I helped Ardrey in his trading at a couple of small villages. The deep hurt inside me was slowly going away, and I was otherwise mending. Of course, I had not forgotten the two nice fellows who had carefully worked me over. I hoped to see them again one fine day in Kikori, and settle a score. But finding Ruyker had top priority at that moment, over any personal grudge.

In late afternoon of the second day, we arrived at Bik Pella. It was not really a town, but just a couple of dirt streets running away from the river, and a general store run by one of the more civilized locals, and some corrugated-iron huts. Nothing but canoes went upriver beyond Bik Pella Post.

I was glad to get off the smelly boat, after two days aboard. The *Princess* was no lady, believe me. She assailed the nostrils with various ugly odors day and night, and her engines pounded heavily on the ear-drums, and she offered almost no comfort to her human cargo. Her only saving grace was that she was an island of comparative safety in the hostile jungle, and now that we were off her, on dry land again, I immediately noticed the sudden absence of her small protection from the wilds around us.

Ardrey knew the Dani local who ran the general store, so we were put up there for the night. The couple of streets of the outpost were crowded with natives wearing kilt-like skirts called lap-laps around their thighs. Dirty children, naked and wild-looking, played happily in the blast-furnace sun, and bare-breasted women carried burdens atop their heads. The men, with their very broad noses and fierce-looking eyes, decorated themselves with ochre dyes, necklaces of boars' tusks, exotic shells from the river, and bird-of-paradise feathers.

I passed an almost sleepless night in a back room of the general store, with Ardrey only a few feet away, snoring loudly on another cot. Torn mosquito netting did not deter the humming insects, and I was glad I had taken my malaria pills. Already, the *Princess* seemed a friendly haven that I would be glad to return to. We could not sleep aboard that night, though, because her engines were being gone over by an employee of the general store proprietor, a good mechanic who would only work on the boat at night, and he made one hell of a racket aboard.

The next morning, at just past dawn, we left the *Papuan Princess* and Bik Pella behind, and headed off into the jungle. We took two of the strongest crewmen with us—a couple of wiry fellows from a coastal tribe with very bushy, wiry hair and decorative scars on their oily bodies—and left the four others to guard the *Princess* against marauders.

I had the crazy idea there might be a track of sorts from Bik Pella Post, for vehicles or at least horses. I was wrong. We headed out on foot, with our porters carrying our provisions on their heads and backs. There was a trail of sorts in the direction of the Bamu villages, but it was so slight in places that it was difficult for Ardrey to keep on it, and he had taken it on a number of previous occasions. I'd fought in the jungle in the recent past, so I was no tenderfoot. But the insects swarmed so fiercely at places that I thought they would drive me out of my head. The heat, damp and sticky, was a real adversary for us, pressing on us at every step. Cockatoos chattered overhead in the high treetops, and there were other noises from the jungle that I could not identify and did not care to.

We were on the trail for sixteen hours that day, and it became a kind of hell before it was over. Finally, at least an hour after dark had fallen over the jungle, we stumbled into the Bamu village.

It was a large one, and on the southeast extremity of what had been, until recently, the extent of the Bamu territory. Since the arrival of the guns to the Kiwais, though, most of the northern villages had been destroyed or evacuated, and now the big chief, Merah, had made this village his home base.

There were several fires lighted inside the village perimeter, and we had been expected. We had heard the tattoo of the hollow-log warning system from a mile away. Now we were met by children and women as we entered the rows of thatched huts on high, dry ground, and the women were chanting a weird, tuneless welcome on either side of us. At the center of the village stood the broad, stocky figure of Nanabe Merah, sporting a headdress and cloak of brilliant bird-of-paradise feathers that shone vibrant in the firelight. Beside him stood a taller fellow behind a grotesque carved wooden mask, who, I learned later, was Zigibi, Merah's big priest. Flanking the two of them were Merah's many village warriors, carrying axes and machetes and spears and looking deadly. To one side, near a kind of community hut, were stacked a dozen of the German Volkssturm rifles I had sold to Ruyker in Sydney, on the far side of the universe. I caught Ardrey's eye, and he nodded.

"Ah!" Merah said loudly to us as we stopped before him and his grand assemblage. "Mr. Ardrey. It be too-long sunrise after we look-see-face on each. You well-coom."

The chanting had stopped and the women were moving into the village behind us. There were odors infiltrating my nostrils that I had never, ever smelled before, and most of them were decidedly unpleasant.

"Bloody good to see you again, Merah!" Ardrey grinned, looking more ragged than a Baghdad beggar, and showing the missing tooth hole in his mouth.

"You come for too-long stay, heh, make-happy with Merah's gorls?"

"No women or booze on this trip, Big Bamu," Ardrey shook his head. "Big bik pella business. Mr. Rainey here comes all the way from Port Morseby to speak with Merah."

All eyes were suddenly on me. "Glad to meet you, Great Merah, chief of all the Bamu," I greeted him. I had been coached by Ardrey.

Merah made a sign to me, and the priest behind the grotesque wooden mask eyed me hostilely through the eye-holes. The warriors standing around us with the long shields and weapons looked about as fierce as any *homo sapiens* I had ever encountered, and I had seen some wild ones, in Africa and South America. Several men wore slivers of bone through their noses and lower lips, and one sported a ball-point pen driven through the bottom of a very large nose—taken, possibly, from some missionary or trader who had fallen out of favor.

"You honor our village," Merah told me in an also-rehearsed phrase, and the only real English I had heard from him. "You talk-sit with machine-make-smoke, we make big arrows from head."

I had no idea what the hell he was talking about, but when he turned and headed for the big community hut with its four open sides, and Ardrey beckoned for me to follow, I did.

Now I got a chance to look around the firelit village, and it was a revelation. The huts that sheltered the Bamus were only lean-tos, and crude ones at that. The villagers slept on grass beds under those shelters, like animals, and ugly odors came from some of them. Around the village in various places stood tall poles, and the decorations on top of them caught my eye immediately. They were human heads, freshly cut off their victims. A couple of them still dripped blood. The eyes were half-open in some of them, and the mouth ajar, so that it appeared the head was staring in surprise at its new surroundings.

I had never seen a trophy pole before, nor a human head used as decoration to brighten up a village.

Just outside the big hut we entered, there was a fire with a spit over it, and a woman tended the cooking. On the spit was a long piece of meat, and when I looked at it closely, I saw that it was a human thigh. At another fire, one that had almost gone out, there were remnants of bones that looked very human.

Ardrey saw me staring, and nudged me in the ribs, and I followed him on into the hut.

Inside, we squatted cross-legged in a circle, with only the chief Merah, Zigibi behind his wild-looking mask, and three elders taking part. The hut, though, was ringed by warriors. Merah lighted a short, thin pipe made of green bamboo, and smoked some dry-looking twigs in it, and passed it around. Ardrey insisted I give it a try, and the inhalation of the smoke from those twigs almost asphyxiated me on the spot. I coughed some, and Merah grinned broadly and seemed to enjoy it. Zigibi said something in Bamu into Merah's ear, and the palaver began.

Merah gave up on his pidgin English at that talk, and reverted to Bamu, because Ardrey knew the dialect fairly well. I sat there and listened, with the weird-looking Zigibi never taking his eyes off me. I wondered if he were coveting my head. Ardrey kept talking in the strange-sounding language to Merah, and would turn to me from time to time and translate. Yes, Ruyker had been there. Merah had been advised by Zigibi to roast Ruyker alive when he showed up a few days ago with his porters, but when he offered to sell Merah guns to match the weaponry that the Kiwais and Motu Kokoda already owned, and had terrorized the Bamus with, Merah had decided to deal as his only chance for survival.

Ardrey turned to me and translated the last part of that, and I nodded. "Tell him that the rifles are more of a danger to him than to Kokoda," I said to Ardrey. "Say that they will cause a war that will wipe out the Bamus, who are inferior in number to the Kiwais. Tell him I'll buy the rifles back from him, and that I also intend to buy back those that Ruyker has left, and those Kokoda uses against Merah's people."

There was a rather lengthy dialogue then, during which Merah scowled toward me a couple of times, as he spoke in his dialect. There was also some animated haranguing of Merah by his priest Zigibi. When it was over, Ardrey turned his grizzled face to me solemnly.

"He says the Bamu are ravaged by recent Kiwai attacks and raids. They are in mourning at this moment because of many deaths in a recent battlefield encounter in which rifles were used with devastating effect against them. I gather the body count on the Bamu side was bloody high. He says he won't give up his new rifles unless we disarm Kokoda."

I sighed heavily. Merah had understood some of Ardrey's translation, and now nodded his affirmation firmly. "Yes. Is end-talk on same," he added soberly. He spoke to Ardrey again in dialect, and Ardrey turned to me.

"He says his people need instruction in the use of the guns. Ruyker showed them how they work, but they need training. He says, until such time as you disarm Kokoda, he will need instruction for his warriors, and asks if you can help."

I shook my head negatively. "I'm in the business of disarming them at this point," I said. "That's the only authority I have from Canberra. I think the authorities would find it counterproductive to train Bamus in the use of the rifle."

I could tell that Ardrey did not like the task of telling Merah that. But I had no choice. As things stood at the moment, my mob was to find Ruyker and try to de-escalate all of this somehow. Ardrey told Merah, and Merah scowled. Zigibi yelled out what must have been an obscenity, and jumped to his feet, pointing a bony dark finger toward me. He was about to "point the bone," put a black-magic hex on me. But Merah stopped him with a single harsh command.

"You go look-see Kokoda," Merah told me seriously. "You no take fire-sticks from, we make war with same."

I got the message. "It's a deal," I told him.

We decided to stay overnight in the community hut, in sleeping bags, in preference to the individual huts that Merah generously offered us. Our porters were treated even more like outsiders than we were, and slept beside us in the open-sided shelter. It was a mile-long night, with soaring mosquitoes and blood-sucking flies and all manner of crawling things on the ground and in the thatch over our heads. When dawn finally came, I had been up an hour, making myself a hot cup of coffee and trying not to look at what remained in the low-flickering fires nearby.

The trophy poles were even more gruesome in the daylight, and big flies buzzed continuously on them. I ignored them, too, and helped Ardrey and the two porters re-pack and prepare for the trek into the jungle toward the Tolai village about a half-day's hike to the east, where Ruyker was believed to have gone. Our plan was to leave in late morning, and hope to arrive at the Tolai village by dark that same day. But the best-laid plans seem to go awry when you least expect it.

We were within fifteen minutes of leaving, when it all happened. There was a short, excited warning from a warrior out on the perimeter of the jungle, and then a scream from him, and it started. We were suddenly in the middle of a Kawai raid.

It had been timed beautifully, because Merah had sent a large part of his warrior unit out in mid-morning, to make sure the way was safe for Ardrey and me. Now the Kiwais, taking advantage of that temporary weakness of the Bamu village, came swarming into it like dogs from hell. By the time Ardrey and I really knew what was happening, they had penetrated into the center of the village, killing and maiming with axes and spears, but mostly with Ruyker's rifles. The clatter of the gunfire was ominous in that primitive village, a sound I wish I had never heard.

Immediately the Bamus went for their own small stack of rifles, but not one was fired. None of them knew how to handle the guns, and were shot down or beheaded with the steel axes before they could respond to the attack. Women and children were struck down impartially and more viciously than the warriors, and I saw a couple of the younger women being carried off. There were bloody corpses lying everywhere within just minutes, and mutilated-but-living Bamus, with arms or legs gone, or their middles sliced through. The ones who were shot were frequently hit in the head —a favorite Kiwai target, apparently—and there were a lot of skulls exploded, gray matter and bone spattered over the ground. The din of the rifles was loud in our ears, and the screams of the Bamus and Kiwais. The Kiwais looked almost exactly like the Bamus, except that they appeared a slightly more handsome people, and perhaps a bit cleaner-looking. Their warriors were not much more than shoulder-high on me—the same as the Bamus—but they were muscular and fierce-looking. They killed wantonly and with obvious pleasure, and they did it all very efficiently.

The Bamus were fighting back after the first couple of minutes, and were giving a good account of themselves with their axes and spears. Several Kiwais were run through very near me, one of them just after he had blown the side of a Bamu's face off with a Volkssturm rifle. Merah and Zigibi were in the middle of it all, with warriors all around them. Zigibi, without his mask, looked almost as frightening as with it, and I saw him kill three Kiwais within thirty seconds with a specially-made broad-bladed axe that these tribes used as both tools and weapons. Merah tried to fire a Volkssturm, failed, and bashed a Kiwai skull in with the stock of the weapon. Ardrey and I had drawn sidearms—I brought the Star .45 into play immediately—and were going for the Kiwais with rifles, and hitting a lot of them. I saw Ardrey hit by a rifle slug in the left arm, and go down to one knee, and almost simultaneously one of his two porters was beheaded with one swift stroke of a Kiwai axe, his head toppling to the ground and rolling into the dying fire nearby.

"Get out of here, Merah!" Ardrey shouted now, from a kneeling position on the bloody ground. *"There are too many of the bloody bastards!"*

Ardrey was kneeling near the burnt-out fire outside the big hut, and I was about twenty feet away, beside our gear. Just after his shout toward Merah, a Kiwai came up behind him and jammed a spear through his torso, back to front. I saw the bloody tip come out through his shirt as his eyes went wide. I fired and knocked the Kiwai down, and then another raced up and severed Ardrey's head with two chopping strokes of a machete-type knife.

I was stunned. From the corner of my eye, I could see Merah and Zigibi retreating now into the jungle at the edge of the village, to keep from being killed. Warriors were retreating with them, and the few women that were still unharmed. Ardrey's other porter, a small, wiry fellow, was shot in the neck as he bent over Ardrey's headless body, and his spine was severed by the shot, his head whip-lashing on his shoulders as he hit the dust of the compound.

"Jesus!" I muttered to myself.

I turned to fire at an approaching Kiwai, when another one came up on my blind side and aimed a Volkssturm at my face and squeezed on the trigger. The gun did not go off. He had probably shot himself out of ammunition. Before I could aim the Star at him, he swung the barrel of the gun across the side of my head, and it cracked loudly there, and I thumped hard on the ground, dazed and bleeding.

I expected to die horribly in those next seconds, but I did not. The shouting and screaming had died down, and most of the firing had stopped. I felt rough hands roll me onto my chest, and bind my hands and feet, and then I passed out for a brief time. When I came around, I was being jogged down a jungle path away from the Bamu village. I was being carried on a pole, hanging down from it like a freshly-killed piece of game, a Kiwai warrior on either end.

I had been taken alive, and was obviously being carried back to the Kiwai village for some grisly ritual, the nature of which I did not dare even contemplate.

THREE

The more aware I became, on that trip back to the dark center of the Kiwai territory, the more of a nightmare it was. The bonds on my wrists and ankles supported my entire weight as I hung from that pole between the warriors, and bit deeply into my bruised flesh, making me yell in anguish at first, and then becoming numb as I lost feeling in the extremities.

I was carried that way for hours, with only one rest stop, when a Kiwai with muscular shoulders and an overpowering stench about him forced some sour liquid down my throat that I almost threw back up. Mosquitoes swarmed on me and flies chewed on the wounds made by the vine-ropes. It was an ugly hell that seemed as if it would never end, and I knew very well that when I got to that village, things would only get worse. I would most certainly lose my head in a very violent way. But, before that happened, they might decide to have some fun with me. And I could not even guess at the rituals that might occur to their primitive minds.

Finally, in mid-afternoon, we arrived at our destination. We were a half-mile-long column of maybe a hundred warriors, with a few women captives and me. The village was a large one, covering several hundred yards in width, and we were met with a throng of screaming, chanting women and children. As I was carried into the village, dogs bit at my back, dark-skinned children beat on me with sticks, and women spat into my face. At the center of the village, near a large community hut not unlike the one we had slept in, in the Bamu village, I was dumped unceremoniously onto the ground, and cut loose from the pole. In doing so, the warrior assigned to the task came close to hacking one of my wrists open. I fell onto my side then, just waiting for the next atrocity.

There were more attacks now from the children and women, who came up one at a time, a little fearfully, and kicked me in the back and side, or hit at me with heavy sticks. The men who had brought me back alive got a big laugh out of this. Some of them had the German VK-98 rifles slung over their naked shoulders, and I wished I had never gotten involved with the damnable weapons, or ever heard of Hendrik Ruyker.

A rather tall Kiwai—almost as tall as me— came out from the big hut, decorated with more luxuriant plumage than the warriors, and shook some kind of dust over me, and I figured he was Zigibi's counterpart at this headquarters of the Kiwai. He muttered some unintelligible words over me, and then barked some commands to a couple of warriors, and they grabbed me by the arms and began dragging me away from the hut.

"Hey!" I protested, being dragged through the dust. *"Wait! Let me talk to Kokoda!"*

But they did not listen. I was dragged along roughly, with children running, yelling alongside, to the edge of a pit over beside another rather large hut. At the edge of the pit I was able to look down inside it before they threw me in, and I saw the big, ugly male monkeys there. There were a half-dozen of them, and they looked almost as big as Chacma baboons I had seen in East Africa. They also looked thin—therefore hungry—and very tense and irritated.

I swallowed hard. *"Look, damn it. I have to talk to Kokoda. He just may not want me dead. Is he here? I want—"*

In the next instant, while I was still babbling, trying to save my skin, two warriors rolled me into the pit.

It was a ten-foot drop, and I hit on my feet first, fortunately, and then thumped hard on my side. There was a loud screaming and yelling by the monkeys around me, who now looked like gorillas, from my new vantage point. I lay there wracked with pain, gasping from the trauma of the fall, while the monkeys circled around me warily, and the Kiwai shouted encouragement at them from above.

I slowly got my breath back, and focused on the monkeys. I saw now, when they grimaced toward me, that they had canine teeth over an inch long. The animals stood almost two feet high on their back legs, and they looked mean as hell. One rushed in and bit at my thigh tentatively, tearing a piece out of my trousers. I yelled and drew my leg toward me, and saw the spot of blood there. Another monkey rushed up and tore savagely at my foot, but only ripped my shoe open. Two more came in toward my face and head, and I hit out at them wildly. One gashed my face with a claw before I could defend against him.

Up at the top of the pit, the sun burned down and the faces of kids and women and some men showed in a tight ring, and they were really enjoying the show. I had no time to get my back up about their cruelty, though. Another monkey came in and tried to take part of my arm away with him.

This time I caught the bushy-faced anthropoid in a frenzied death grip, around its throat, and squeezed. It kicked and bit to get away, but I was strong in my desperation. I choked off its wind completely, and it kicked more feebly, and then quit. I dropped it onto the hard ground beside me, and the others stared at it, the chattering and growling not so loud, now. I pulled the shoe off that one of them had loosened, and held it by the toe, so that I might wield the heel end as a club. Up above me, in that circle of hard sunlight, the Kiwais had fallen silent. I held the shoe and crouched there on my heels, watching that moving group of animals assess me again. In a brief moment, the biggest of them came in again, toward my thigh. I swung wildly and the hard heel of the shoe connected with its skull. It yelled raucously and hit the dirt on its side, kicking the dust up, then fell motionless. A third monkey, seemingly enraged by this, came in screaming like a demon, going for my throat. I smashed the shoe against its face as it came, and the jaw fractured loudly. The monkey bounded off me and then fell onto its side, screeching loudly in new pain.

"Come on, damn you!" I growled to the rest of them. "Did you lose your appetites?"

The remaining three monkeys now shrunk back

on their side of the pit, huddling together there and listening to the yowls of the last one I had downed. I raised the shoe above my head in a warning gesture, and they pressed even further away from me.

I had become king of the pit.

This was extremely disappointing to the Kiwais who had thrown me down there to see me torn slowly to shreds by the razor teeth of the beasts who inhabited the pit. There was complete silence up above now, and in the midst of it, a new head appeared up there. It wore a big, fancy headdress of feathers, and its broad face scowled arrogantly down at me. Beside it was the face of the priest who had ordered my grisly entertainment for the locals.

"Are you Kokoda?" I yelled up to the face, weakly.

There was no reply.

"If you are, I want to speak with you," I said loudly. *"About Hendrik Ruyker."*

The face went away, and the priest's went with it. I figured it had to be Kokoda. I waited down there, keeping an eye on the remaining monkeys. The yells of the busted-jaw one had died down, and he had crawled over to where the other three still hunched together against the far dirt wall, eyeing me furtively. In a moment there was some conversation from above, and then a rope ladder plunged down into the pit, beside me.

I stared at it for a moment, then rose and showed the shoe to the monkeys. They understood. I turned and headed up the ladder, the shoe still in hand. The monkeys seemed relieved to see me leave.

When I got to the top, two warriors roughly took me in tow again, binding my wrists almost as tightly as they had been before. Then I was pushed and prodded with spears and rifle muzzles to the big hut with the open sides at the center of the village. Under the shade of the structure sat the rather tall fellow with the fancy headdress, on a reed pallet. Beside him, now wearing a wooden mask even more weird than Zigibi's at the Bamu village, was the priest, whose name I later found to be Titimua. Also sitting there were several older-looking men, obviously village elders. They looked like something out of a Hollywood horror film.

I was shoved to a sitting position by my guards, and then the fellow with the fancy headdress spoke.

"Yes. I am Kokoda," he told me.

I was amazed by his command of English, in comparison to Merah of the Bamus. "I am Rainey," I told him. "I came to find Ruyker. But your warriors found my party at a Bamu village, and killed my friend Ardrey and his men."

He made no apology about Ardrey. "I lived in Bik Pella Post when a child. A missionary taught me your language. I speak well, yes?"

I nodded. "Yes."

"Why are you in a Bamu village?"

"I came looking for Hendrik Ruyker. I want to buy his rifles," I explained.

His broad face was slightly more handsome than Merah's—if there is handsomeness in that area—and he was taller and more muscularly built than Merah and most Bamus. In fact, the Kiwais in general looked better-nourished than the

Bamus. "You come to the jungle to buy rifles? You may do so in Kikori."

"You don't understand," I told him. "I sold Ruyker all these guns. I have been asked by the Canberra government to buy them back. So you and others will not kill each other with them."

His dark face was somber. His priest Titimua leaned toward me, behind the mask. *"You sell Bamus guns!"*

I was surprised that he, too, spoke some English. I shook my head sidewise. "No, I tried to buy those back. Ruyker sold the guns to them."

They were all silent, trying to read my face. Finally, Kokoda spoke. "I believe you, Rainey. It is clear you and Ruyker must both die."

"What?" I said.

"He, because he sells guns now to our enemies. You, because you would interfere in Kiwai matters."

I swallowed hard. He had no intention of saving me from his tribe's grim rituals. Kokoda was not civilized, just because he spoke English. He reached behind him and picked up a fancy rifle I had not noticed before, a British Enfield 7.62 mm Envoy, with silver inlaid into its dark mahogany stock. It was a beautiful gun, and it had not come from the cache I sold Ruyker. Kokoda held it above shoulder level now, in true warrior style.

"This will make me chief of all," Kokoda said in his staccato English. "I do not recognize the Canberra bik pella, or the authority at Port Moresby. There will be one big tribe, and Kokoda will rule it."

"After murdering thousands of men, women and children who defend themselves with spears?"

I suggested.

Kokoda grunted. "Do not try to understand how it is between the Kiwai and others," he told me. "Your beautiful head is good for only one thing, and we will make good use of it."

He nodded to his warriors standing behind me, and before I could protest, they dragged me to my feet and started hauling me away. The priest Titimua yelled after me. *"You look-see from trophy pole, Rainey!"*

They took me out into the hot sun again, and tied me to a post out in the center of an open area. I could see the entire village from there, and I now noticed the trophy poles standing all around the place. There was one above the community hut, and now my jaw dropped open slightly when I saw the head stuck on its fifteen-foot top. It was Burke Ardrey, complete with grizzled beard on his chin and weathered, tanned flesh. The eyes were closed, but somehow there was still a look of surprise on the lifeless face.

"Jesus H. Christ!" I muttered.

I turned away from the bloody, grisly sight. Not far away, some almost-naked women were building a fireplace with dirt embankments around it, and a spit over it. They kept looking toward me and giggling, their pendulous breasts swinging in the sun. Except for the breasts, it was difficult to tell the women from the men. They all were grime-encrusted, and most wore painted decorations on their bodies, and shell jewelry that hung from their necks and waists. The men had wild, kinky hair that stood out from their heads several inches, and many had a bone sliver or other adornment thrust through the bottom of their noses. Several men came up to examine my face and hair closely, as if looking over a piece of merchandise at a market. There was an empty trophy pole very near the community hut, and this was being re-decorated by an elderly Kiwai while the others worked at other tasks. I figured that was where my head would end up. It was not a comforting thought.

Kokoda left the village in late afternoon with a group of warriors, but I had the idea he would return in time for the ceremony they were building toward, in the evening, in which I would be the featured entertainment. When Kokoda was gone, the ugly priest Titimua came and stood very close to me, and I could smell his rancid breath in my face. He spoke to me in Kiwai, and I did not understand a word of it. Then he took out a pouch of bone fragments and other small, odd-looking objects, and threw them into a heap on the ground at my feet. He repeated the process, studying the bits and pieces. Then he rose and stared into my face again. He said something quite lengthy in Kiwai, and then added in English, "The gods talk-say you die slow-slow. I make-do."

"Go pick your foot-wide nose," I told him.

He did not understand, and that was just as well. He went off to show the women how to prepare the outdoor grill for leg-of-Rainey, while I contemplated my abbreviated future. I figured by midnight that night I would have died in a pretty ugly way, and there seemed to be damned little I could do about it.

After Titimua left, a small knot of women came up to me, with children in tow, and one ugly female jagged me in the groin with a stick. I yelled and she loved it, and she repeated it several times. A warrior came up and drove them off—I presume he did not want them to spoil the meat—and proceeded to test the sharpness of a small axe blade on my chest, after tearing my shirt open. He sliced into flesh with the razor-sharp blade, and I hissed in pain, but he did not seem to notice or care.

As darkness fell I was left alone while further preparations were made for the big ceremony later. No real guard was put on me, but all the warriors watched me closely. My hands had been tied with vine-rope again, and to the head-high post then. It bit deeply into the flesh there, making the earlier rope-wounds worse, and giving me fits before the darkness set in. In early evening, before Kokoda's return, the preliminaries began.

They brought out a couple of female prisoners from Merah's village, women I had forgotten they carried away, and they tied one of them up hand and foot, then slung her onto a spit over the fireplace—which as yet had no fire built in it—and then trussed her up into a kind of ball around the spit, like a big chunk of beef. She did some yelling through that, and nobody listened. Then they began smearing her with red mud from a big pot, plastering her with the stuff over and over again, until she soon resembled a big mud ball on the spit. Something clammy grabbed at me inside my gut as I realized that they were preparing her for cooking—alive.

That was one of the rituals practiced by these people to whom Ruyker had sold modern guns. Another, I had heard, was to lop off pieces of the victim, while alive, to cook over a fire, saving the head until last, which would go atop a trophy pole. I figured that was probably the ritual I was to go through, since my head was obviously a great addition to Kokoda's collection, from the way he had stared at it covetously.

A short length of bamboo had been inserted into the woman's mouth before the mud caked her over completely, so that she could breathe, but not scream. Neither could she move a muscle, under all that rope and mud. She would roast alive, with no capacity to react to it all, except mentally. It was the most barbarous act I had ever seen planned against a human by another, and I had been to some pretty primitive places in the world. The lopping-off butchery, which I figured they had planned for me, to save my head, would not be a hell of a lot nicer.

It was dark now, and drummers gathered in a circle around the place where the big fire would be, and men dancers had put on plumed shoulder-decorations and tied other ones around their ankles. They intended to have a good time. It all turned my stomach.

I knew that I had to free myself somehow soon, if there were going to be any chance for survival. It was all going to start very soon. When Kokoda arrived back, I would be watched more carefully, and opportunity would probably be gone. That meant I had to act immediately.

There seemed to be no way to loosen those bonds at my wrists without severing my hands. There was blood caked there already, and my hands felt numb beyond the wrists. That, I knew, would give me trouble, even if I got free. But I would think of that if the problem arose.

I got an idea, finally, as the Kiwai women prepared to light the fire under the mud-caked Bamu woman. I leaned hard against the post, to test it strength in the ground, and it gave a little.

A flood of hope washed into my chest. I pushed backwards again, and the post moved a couple of inches that time. I pulled forward and it loosened up even more. I took a look around me and saw no one looking toward me. I shoved to my right, and the post gave even more. I was just ready to shove the other way, when two young Kiwai boys ran up to me, with a yellow dog. The biggest boy shouted something at me and then began clubbing my shins with a heavy stick, while the other one laughed like hell. The dog took a couple of nips out of my ankles whil this was going on. Three women at the fire pit, about thirty feet away, turned and laughed for a moment, then went back to their work. The boys finally tired of beating me, and ran off toward the women.

I stood there gasping in pain from my shins and ankles, waiting for it all to subside a little. Warriors were gathering near the fire pit and the big hut, now, and time was running out on me. I shoved to my left, and the post almost toppled over with me attached to it.

It was completely free from the hole, ready to be pulled out.

I wondered how far down in the ground it went. Probably not much more than a foot, I figured, from the way it had loosened. I looked around me, and there were Kiwais everywhere. It looked impossible.

Then I got a break. There was a tattoo of log drums from the jungle, a signal that Kokoda was returning.

This caused considerable excitement in the village. Most of the remaining warriors moved off to the far edge of the village, to meet Kokoda when he arrived, and many women went, too. Suddenly I was being ignored totally.

I did not hesitate. With a big step forward, I pulled the post out of the ground. A foot-and-a-half of it came out, and it was free. I stood there bent over then, the post on my back. Nobody had seen me. I dropped to my side, and began pulling the ropes up toward the top of the post. It was slow at first, but then it went more easily. A woman at the fire pit looked toward me, and I was sure I had been discovered. But she must have been thinking of something else, because she just looked back down to her work, without taking any notice of me. I pulled and shoved, and the rope came over the top of the post.

I quickly stood up again, to give the impression I was still tied there. The bonds on my wrists were loose, now. Nobody seemed to be looking. I turned and moved slowly and deliberately to a nearby lean-to hut, and walked around behind it.

I was alone. Out of sight of them.

I pulled my left hand free from the ropes, and then the right. I dropped the bonds to the ground, and massaged my wrists gently. Blood raced back into my hands, giving me sudden and violent pain, the way it does when you warm frozen hands too quickly. I stood there flexing my fingers, gasping in pain. Finally it was better.

I sneaked around to the far side of the community hut, away from the women. Kokoda was now arriving at the far side of the village, and now even the last of the women were getting up from their work and going to meet their chief. I looked around inside the big hut, and noticed that shrunken heads had been placed all around the place, for decoration. A low fire burned in the hut's center, and smoke from it wafted through a hole in the roof. It gave enough light to see by, and I noticed a bamboo box near where Kokoda had sat, that afternoon.

Beside the box sat an elder.

He had sat so motionless that I had not even noticed him. He eyed me with open contempt now, as he rose and turned to give the alarm. I came up behind him, threw an arm over his head, and closed it on his skinny neck. He thrashed about in my arms, and then was lifeless.

He fell like a rag doll to my feet.

I looked outside, and saw that nobody had seen or heard our small struggle. Going to the box, I opened it and found my Star .45 in there, and the pistol Ardrey had carried. I grabbed the Star, which was fully loaded, and stuck it into my belt. There was a Volkssturm rifle propped against the hut wall near the box. I grabbed it, checked its ammo, and grabbed a cartridge box lying nearby. I was ready to leave.

Outside the hut hanging over the unlighted fire was the Bamu woman, encased in mud and bound into a ball. Nobody was tending her at the moment. I knew I did not have the ability to save her, but I could not help thinking of how she was to die. I stepped out into the night, crept up to the spit on which she hung, and found her head under all that clay. On the ground nearby lay a steel axe. I picked it up, turned its flat end down, and swung the blunt instrument against that lump of clay. There was a sudden but almost unnoticeable shudder under all that drying mud, and then crimson seeped from the bashed-in place.

I had killed her.

The other Bamu woman had been killed unceremoniously, so there was no one left at the moment for them to practice their unnatural acts upon. I turned and started to run like hell.

There was a shout from the opposite side of the compound.

I turned and looked, and a warrior was pointing toward me, and gesturing wildly. Kokoda, right behind him, had an ugly look on his dark face. Kokoda shouted something, and fifty Kiwais yelled like demons from Hades and came racing toward me.

My escape had been discovered.

FOUR

Kneeling quickly in the infantry firing position, I aimed down the barrel of the VK-98 and squeezed the trigger. The closest Kiwai warrior yelled and plummeted onto his face, his heart exploded.

The others all stopped momentarily, staring at their dead companion in shock. They had never seen such deadly firing of the rifle at that range. They were obviously amazed by how quickly I had killed with it, and a couple of them looked afraid. It was one thing to kill with guns—another to be killed. I aimed and fired again, and another wild-looking Kiwai was hit, jumping backwards and hitting the ground on his back. This one, though, kicked and flailed in the dirt for a moment, before he finally lay lifeless.

There was some muttering from the warriors, and a couple of women screamed. Kokoda, enraged suddenly, yelled savagely at his warriors to kill me. A couple of them responded, and then others.

Only a couple of them had rifles, and they seemed reluctant to use them until they were very close to me. I fired again, the rifle banging out loudly in the jungle night, and a third Kiwai went down. Then I turned and ran like hell.

In just seconds I reached the trees. A shot came banging after me as I plunged into the forest, and I kept going. When I had made a hundred yards, I stopped and could hear them crashing through the underbrush after me. I turned and kept going.

It was pitch black in those trees. I stumbled along awkwardly, crashing into underbrush and tree trunks and falling several times. I was heading for the path they had brought me to the village over, and in that darkness I almost missed it. After ten minutes of plunging along in the blackness, I ran across it and into the trees again, realized then what I had done, and circled back to it.

There were at least three Kiwais right behind me. They knew the jungle around them, and they were in better shape than me, on my best day. But I was weak from their treatment of me, and I knew I could not outrun the best of them. As I made my way stumblingly along the trail, I heard them coming closer. I ducked into some trees at the edge of the trail, and crouched there perfectly quiet.

They came rushing past, not one seeing me. There were four of them. Any others still in the chase had taken alternate chase routes. When the last man ran past, I stepped out behind him and shot him in the back.

The Kiwai yelled loudly and plunged, falling, into the trees to his right. The next-to-last man, still only thirty paces up the trail, turned quickly. I could just make him out. He raised his rifle to fire at me, and I beat him. There was another cracking report from my gun, and he jerked sidewise as if a liana noose had pulled at his head. He went down and out of sight, but I knew I had hit him dead-center.

I now circled off the trail while the others turned and came back. They were more cautious now, and I heard dark mutterings as they discovered both companions. They returned along the path slowly, not having learned yet how dangerous a jungle path can be, with modern weapons against you. I waited until they had both passed me, then crashed out onto the path behind them again. When I aimed this time, though, the closest man was not so visible. The rifle cracked loudly and I missed him. He fired back with his Volkssturm, and my right arm felt as if a red-hot poker had been run across the outer aspect of the biceps. I squeezed down on the trigger again, and the hammer clicked on an empty chamber.

The rifle was out of ammunition, and I had no time to re-load. I drew the Star automatic and fired three times in rapid succession at the shadow on the path. There was a dull yell from there, and a thump on the ground. In the next instant, I saw the motion beside me, out of the corner of my eye.

The last Kiwai had used some strategy of his own. He had flanked me while I shot it out with his comrade, and now, with only a short-handled steel axe as a weapon, he was hurling himself at me from the underbrush, the axe blade arcing toward my neck to decapitate me.

I jerked backwards at the last split-second, and the small axe sliced through the collar of my bush jacket, just nicking the flesh underneath. I stumbled and started falling, but grabbed the arm of the Kiwai as I went, and we plummeted to the jungle path together.

We rolled over and over there in that darkness, with me trying to get the Star in action and the Kiwai straining to free his arm so that he might split me in two with that axe. I could just barely make out his heavy, wild features as he rolled on top of me, the blood-shot eyes psychotic-looking, the broad nostrils flared. My left arm trembled with the effort of keeping the axe off me, and I could see its blade glint dully above my head. I turned the Star slowly, against the animal strength of his restraining hand, and pointed the muzzle at his left eye, and squeezed the trigger.

The stubby automatic exploded loudly in our ears, and the slug entered the Kiwai's face through the iris of the left eye, traveled through the frontal lobe of his primitive brain, and exited above his right ear, spraying bone and blood into the foliage beside him. He jumped off me sidewise, crashing into the underbrush, and thrashed in it for just a moment before quitting.

I got up weakly. I had been lucky, getting only a couple of nicks out of all of that. I listened for a moment, and did not hear any other warriors coming. They had not responded yet to the gunfire. I turned and continued on down the dark path, not looking back, only running blindly to put distance between me and the village.

It took me all that night to trek through that jungle to the Bamu village where all of it had begun, and it was a small miracle that I found the right way at all. When I stumbled into the village at dawn, I found that it was deserted. Merah had wisely decided to move his headquarters, after the savage attack on that one.

I had to rest. I went into the big hut where Ardrey and I had spoken at length with Merah and his priest Zigibi, and it all looked different. It was a shambles. There were no dead bodies around. Merah had removed them, and the thought occurred to me that maybe these people ate their own kind. It was only one small last step from eating their neighbors.

I slept fitfully for a couple of the early morning hours, with jungle noises abruptly waking me on a couple of occasions. Then I took a gourd of water from a nearby hut, checked my Star for ammo and found I had two cartridges left, and headed out again—this time for Bik Pella Post.

It was a long, ugly day, worse in many ways than the night had been. The insects had been worse at night, but now the heat got to me. Sweat ran off me in rivulets, stinging and burning the many insect welts that now covered my flesh. But I kept going, knowing I had to cover ground faster than Ardrey and I had, to get there to the river by dark. It seemed to go on forever. I stopped only for moments at a time, when I felt ready to collapse. Then I kept going. Afternoon came, and then late afternoon. The trail got better and I appreciated the extra ease of movement. Finally, at just dusk in early evening, I reached the river and Bik Pella Post.

I had never been so glad to see anything in my life. I stumbled into the general store that was just closing, and the aborigine proprietor stared hard at me, surveying my torn clothing, the welts all over me, and the caked blood.

"Good heavens, Mr. Rainey!"

"The Kiwais," I mumbled, collapsing heavily

onto a straight chair as villagers gathered outside the open front entrance of the place. "Ardrey and the porters are dead."

He fixed up one of the cots for me again, in the back room, and sent for the head boy from the *Papuan Princess*. Later, in the dim light from a kerosene lantern, while the proprietor tended my small wounds, I told the whole story to them. I also told the aborigine first mate of the *Princess* that I wanted to take the boat back to Kikori the very next morning, and he agreed. There was terror in his dark eyes, and in the eyes of all the rather civilized villagers at the outpost. They were thinking, I knew, that Kokoda could do anything, if he could kill Ardrey and terrorize me—if he could attack white men with impunity. At any moment, he might appear with his armed warriors at Bik Pella Post, to kill and ravage.

I could not have argued the point.

Two days later I was back in Kikori, sitting in Averill Connors' white-washed little office at his post compound, with the small sounds of civilization outside his louver-shuttered window. Connors was somber after my report, because Burke Ardrey had been a friend and bridge companion for years. In a place like Kikori, there were not many white men you found an affinity for, so I felt for Connors.

"Kokoda wasn't there when Ardrey was killed," I finally ended my report to him. "But I doubt that it would have made any difference. There was no apology for the head atop the big hut, that night. And he had absolutely no compunction about killing me. Kokoda has taken on the whole white man's world in New Guinea, Connors. He told me plainly that he no longer recognizes your authority over him. With the rifles, that makes him dangerous."

"Decidedly so," Major Connors said heavily.

"And now I've had to return without even finding Ruyker," I went on. "I've accomplished nothing."

Connors looked up at me. "Well, Rainey, maybe you've gotten lucky, finally."

"In what way?" I asked doubtfully.

"I just heard today that Ruyker is back here already. Ordinarily he would have stayed out in the jungle for weeks on end. Maybe the Kiwai killing of Ardrey scared him some. He would have heard of it by way of the jungle grapevine."

"Do you know where he's at?" I asked.

"Not yet," Connors said. "I was going to send a man around town to look for him, when you arrived."

"I'll find him," I said. "Maybe we can at least stop this where it's at now." I rose, still hurting in several places. "I'll get back to you later, this evening. Maybe I'll have something for you this time."

"I'll be waiting," Connors said.

It was almost dusk when I left Connors' office. I had rented the Land Rover again, and now I drove across town to the girl Nellie Waki's place. I did not find her at home. I drove on to the Owens Guest House at dark, where Ruyker had stayed on a previous visit, and the owner had not seen him since then.

Frustrated, I returned to the flea-bag Goroka Hotel to clean up and go out for a light evening meal. I was just about ready to leave again, when Nellie showed up at my door.

She had recovered from her beating at the hands of Ruyker's business associates, and was looking pretty in a tight-fitting gay-print dress.

"Well," I smiled.

"I got your message," she said, "and came right away-quick."

I let her in, and closed the door behind her. She looked around the room, then turned to me. "I miss you, Rainey. I am hot for you."

I grinned, wondering where she had learned that expression. I was wearing only my trousers, because I had just finished washing up. She ran her brown hands over my chest, and then unfastened my trousers. "I think about you all-time, make-start fire inside me." She already had found me, inside my trousers.

"Nellie—" I protested. She was caressing me steadily. "I'm in a hell of a shape. I've been bitten by wild monkeys, beat on by wild women, and shot at. All I want is rest and—"

I looked down, and she smiled at the success of her first efforts. She knelt before me and continued doing nice things. I forgot how lousy I felt. She hugged me to her and used her mouth expertly.

"Good God," I muttered. "Okay, you win."

I pulled her to her feet and took her to the iron bed in the corner of the room. Over the bed was a faded print of Queen Elizabeth of England. I hoped the Queen did not mind. Nellie pulled her dress off in a mild frenzy, and then came and rolled onto me, pressing me onto my back.

"I do. You rest, Rainey."

Who could refuse an invitation like that? Her firm breasts hung over me in perfect arcs, and her hot tongue found my mouth now, and through all of that she managed an awkward union, sitting astride me. She settled on me nicely, and the sensation brought a ragged gasping to her throat that momentarily filled the room with its soft sound. Then she was making it happen, moving with precision at first, and then, later, with the same wild abandon she had exhibited on that other, first occasion, and it all climaxed, finally, in a surging, hot explosion of carnal fulfillment that was just as violent and primitive as before.

In all the excitement, she tore loose a bandage on my right arm and made a new wound on my shoulder with her long nails.

I did not complain.

When she lay beside me, satiated, later, I asked her if she had seen Ruyker since his return to Kikori.

"Oh, yes," she said casually. "I look-see today. He want to see tomorrow. Now I turn-machine-in-head over same, maybe not go. You know why." She gave me a wide grin.

I returned it. "Where is he staying tonight?" I asked her.

"There is house-give-room on the road he called Epinery. You find-see there."

Nellie wanted to stay and do it all over again, but I had Ruyker on my mind, then. I shooed her off, then took the Land Rover out on Epinery road, on the muddy river. There was a two-story colonial house out there, run by a half-caste aborigine like Nellie, and Ruyker had taken a room upstairs, at the rear of the place. He was there.

When he opened the door and saw me, his hard eyes narrowed down slightly.

"Rainey," he said incredulously.

"Ruyker," I replied. "I'd like to talk with you."

He grunted. "I thought you were out in the bush with Ardrey. I kind of figured you had bought it, old man." He spoke English with a Dutch accent. He was a colonial Dutchman from Indonesia, originally. He stepped aside, and I entered the room. He closed the door and regarded me somberly.

"The Kiwai captured me," I said. "But I got lucky, and got away. I was impressed with their arsenal."

He grinned a hard grin, one I had never liked. He was a big fellow, about my height, but maybe ten years older than me. He looked rugged, and he was. His square face bore a scar across his left eye, and part of his right ear was missing. He could tell some tales, I knew. But the experiences out there in the jungle that made such startling cocktail-time tales had done something to Ruyker that nothing could now undo.

"You ought to be, Rainey. They're the Volkssturms you sold me in Sydney."

"I know," I told him. "Have you heard why I'm out here?"

He was still regarding me suspiciously. He wore bush khakis, with a Mauser 7.65 mm Parabellum automatic pistol slung low on his hip, in a fancy leather holster. He looked as dangerous as he was.

"Can't say I have," he told me. "I figured maybe you were out there with Ardrey to give me some retail competition."

I shook my head. "That's not my bag, Ruyker. I fight wars for a living, remember?"

"Then what are you chasing around the interior of New Guinea for?" he said. "There's nothing going on out there that needs a professional like you."

"The authorities in Canberra sent me, Ruyker," I told him. His face changed again, going straight-lined. "They say I did a stupid thing, selling you the VK-98's. I'm inclined to agree. They want me to buy back everything you have left. At a profit to you."

His gray eyes searched my face closely. "And that's why you were running around out there with Ardrey? To try to find me?"

"That's it. I thought you'd be out there for a month or two. Too bad for Ardrey we didn't stay here and wait you out."

"Too bad," Ruyker said in his accent. "But, *het doet er niets toe*. It doesn't matter, he was a rummy, anyway."

I gave Ruyker a hard look. "Some people might not look at it quite that way, Ruyker. Anyway, I'm prepared to offer you a good profit for the Volkssturms you have left. What do you say?"

Ruyker shook his head firmly. "Not a chance, Rainey. The deal we made was final."

I tried to control my temper. "I know that. But what does it matter whether you re-sell them to me, or to the Kiwais?"

"It matters a great deal," Ruyker replied. "I'm not just dealing with the Kiwais now. The Bamus and other tribes surrounding the Kiwais want guns from me now, to defend themselves."

"From the guns you sold to the Kiwais," I said sourly.

"That's right," he said nonchalantly. "I'm into

a big business, Rainey. I get gold ore and copper from the fuzzy-wuzzies, and I'm just started. Nothing you can offer me would induce me to stop in the middle of something so profitable. And that's what Canberra would want, I gather. For me to pull in my horns and just quit."

"Don't you think it's just a little irresponsible to sell modern weapons to primitives like these?" I said in a low voice. "Have you seen the slaughter out there in the jungle, Ruyker? Have you seen what they're doing with their new toys?"

He shrugged. "Who cares, old man? What does it matter whether they kill with spears to eat each other, or with guns? It all comes out the same, in the end."

"The hell it does," I said. "With government intervention, the cannibalism and head-hunting was being controlled to some extent. And the killing was limited, with spears and axes. Now it will be wholesale. And Kokoda just may end up in Port Moresby, with those damned rifles."

Ruyker now glared at me, too. "I don't give a good goddam what they do with those guns. And if you get in my way, Rainey—*wees voorzichtig!* Be careful that you don't get hurt!"

Ruyker had always been an arrogant bastard, but he was becoming insufferable now. I came up close to him, making up my mind about what to do. "Look, you sonofabitch," I growled. "I want those rifles back. If I don't get them for payment, then you and me will take a ride over to Averill Connors' headquarters and have a little private talk with him. Maybe he'll want to relieve you of them in a more forceful way."

"Don't be absurd, Rainey," Ruyker said stiffly.

"I have no intention of talking with Connors or anybody else further about property that is rightfully mine to do with what I please. You should have thought of all this before you sold me the guns. Now I do with them what I want."

"Damn you, Ruyker!" I grunted out, going for the Star in my light-weight suit jacket.

But Ruyker's hand flashed to the Mauser he wore openly on his hip, and he was faster than me. Before I could get the Star out, he was aiming the Mauser at my center chest.

"Go ahead, Rainey," he grinned harshly.

I removed my hand slowly from my jacket. Ruyker reached carefully in and took it from me, and stuffed it into his belt. "You disappoint me, Rainey," he said then, holding the Mauser on me. "For a man in your profession, you seem suddenly extremely naive, to allow the Canberra government to use you in this way. Maybe you have an ulterior motive, I don't know. Maybe you want the gun business for yourself. Whatever your motivations, though, I am finished with you. I don't need you anymore, because I have other suppliers. You can only give me trouble, Rainey, so you must understand that I cannot tolerate your presence here any longer."

"You sound a lot like the savage Kokoda," I told him. "Are you aware that the Kiwais know about your double-dealing with Merah and others, and keep an empty trophy pole ready, with your name on it?"

Ruyker was not impressed. "Well, if Kokoda ever manages to achieve that goal, you won't be around to gloat, Rainey. *Ga door! Langzaam.*" He motioned with the Mauser for me to precede him to the door.

The bastard was going to take me out and kill me in some quiet place, that was clear. "Don't do it, Ruyker," I said. "You're in enough trouble, already."

"Move, Rainey," he growled.

We left the room and descended an outside stairway to the ground. There was a jungly rear grounds to the estate, and then the black river. "Down to the water," he ordered me.

I figured there was about fifty yards of walking between me and an early demise. I moved along in front of Ruyker, the Mauser nudging me in the ribs. I had to do something or it would all be over, with my body floating in the muddy river. We were passing a big shade tree, and I guided us very close to it. When we were right beside it, I made my desperate move.

With a violent movement I swung my left hand down in back of me, between me and Ruyker, and twisting at the same instant, chopped at his right wrist. He saw the movement and fired, but my twisting motion saved me and the slug just tore at my jacket. Then the back of my left hand was connecting hard with his wrist, punching his gunhand away and toward the tree trunk. The gun fired loudly in my ears again, this time the slug grazing my left jacket sleeve, and then Ruyker's gunhand slammed into the tree trunk, as I had planned. The two traumas to it so close together dislodged the Mauser and it slipped from his grasp as he fell against the tree.

I lost my balance, too, and fell to one knee. I looked for the Mauser on the ground, and could not find it.

"Goddam you, you—meddler!" Ruyker gritted out, going now for my Star in his waistband.

I threw myself bodily at Ruyker as he pulled the Star from its resting place and aimed it at my head. My hand slammed against his first with the Star in it just as it now exploded in our ears, and the shot missed my head by a fraction. We now hit the tree together, and then fell to the ground, Ruyker trying to aim the Star at my face. I saw the muzzle swing around and point at my left eye. I jammed hard against it just as his finger whitened over the trigger, and the gun exploded in my ear and I felt powder burns on my cheek. But the slug had just missed. We rolled once, and I put all my strength into jerking hard at the gunhand, and the Star loosened in his grip, but would not break free. He fell away from me against the base of the big tree, aimed the Star at my face, and squeezed the trigger.

But I knew, suddenly, that it was too late. There was a metallic click and no report from the automatic, and I knew that Ruyker had just used up the last of my ammo, on that last shot. I had checked it out after escaping from Kokoda, and had had only two cartridges left.

Ruyker stared hard at the gun for a moment, his face dark with anger because he had not killed me. Then he was struggling to his feet, muttering obscenities as he did so. He hurled the Star at my head in a fit of anger, and I ducked and it missed. I started to get up awkwardly, and his voice stopped me.

"You can't take me without a gun, Rainey."

I hesitated, then fell onto one knee, exhausted. The past week had taken its toll of me, and I knew he was right.

"I'm heading back into the jungle before all you do-gooders descend on me like jackals," he said in a harsh, low voice. "But I warn you, Rainey. Don't follow me. Don't get in my way again."

With that last defiant statement, Ruyker turned and hurried back to the house and around the side of it. Just as I was getting to my feet, I hard the engine of a vehicle start, and knew that Ruyker was taking off for the interior again.

I had failed to abort his bloody trading in death.

But I had survived my encounter with him. At that particular moment, with the powder burns from my own automatic stinging the side of my face, that did not seem such a small thing.

FIVE

It was hot in Kikori the next day. Heat waves rolled upward from corrugated-iron roofs into a brazen sky, and yellow dogs slunk out of the dusty streets and into the shallow shade of buildings, and water boiled out of the radiators of old vehicles that limped and coughed past the hotel. It was one of those days that is almost intolerable to a white man from the civilized world, but that the natives just seem to stoically endure.

I stayed in my bed late that morning, not wanting to go out in it, preferring to try to heal all my cuts and wounds. I needed rest badly. I sent a message to Connors that Ruyker had run off to continue his dirty dealing, and that he probably had more guns to sell the natives. At noon, when I finally walked to the general store to try to find ammunition for the Star .45, Connors found me there.

The proprietor had just found an old box of cartridges for me when Connors came in. It had taken the fellow fifteen minutes to locate my ammo, because the store was so ill-organized. It was dark and cool—relatively—in the place, though, and there was a broad-bladed ceiling fan over the counter. Behind the counter were shelves that stood about half-empty, with dusty canned and bottled goods and stacks of faded cloth. On the walls at the ends of the long room hung tools and hardware, some of it rusty with age already.

"Well, Rainey. I see you're up and about." Connors clapped me on the shoulder lightly.

"No thanks to that sonofabitch Ruyker," I told him. I paid the aborigine proprietor for the ammo, and he made change while I turned to Connors in his suntan uniform. "He was going to murder me, Connors. The bastard is beyond talking with."

"I shouldn't have allowed you to see him alone," Connors said more seriously now. "The whole bloody thing is my fault. I could have sent a couple of men with you. We'd have had control now, if I had."

"It's me they sent to reason with him," I argued. "And it's me that failed."

I got my change, and Connors suggested we step out onto the shaded porch. I followed him out there, and we seated ourselves on two straight chairs against the bhilding wall, and watched the carts and wagons and fuzzy heads pass by on the street.

"We've had more bad news, I'm afraid, Rainey," Connors said to me, after he had lighted a long cigarette and I had declined one. "Kokoda has wiped out a Tolai village since you escaped from him. Murdered every man, woman and child. Ruyker had sold the tribe some guns and ammunition, and Kokoda took it all. He's doing the same to every village where Ruyker has been. He's calling his people an army now, and says he'll control the whole of Papua before this is over, and challenge the white man's governorship f New Guinea."

"Kokoda just might drive you right out of here, Major," I suggested. "By force. Can you imagine what kind of life those natives under his rule would have? They would never know when they might end up on Kokoda's dinner table."

Connors sighed heavily. "I don't mind admitting, Rainey, that I'm a little scared," he said, staring out at the street. "With Ruyker on the loose again, passing out guns to those savages as if they were CARE packages, we could be in bad trouble very quickly. And I have no authority to go in after Kokoda with troops. Canberra would never allow it. It's too touchy a thing in world politics. Brutal imperialists abusing their power, and all that. There are well-meaning politicos in Canberra and London both who can't understand why we don't give over the bloody government here to the fuzzies. With Kokoda still sitting down to a meal of human leg regularly, and dreaming of our heads as decorations on his trophy poles."

I sat there and considered all that for a long moment, then turned to Connors. "Maybe it's time you took the bull by the horns, and went in and tried to stop Kokoda, before it's too late. Ruyker is on borrowed time. It's Kokoda, now, that you have to take seriously. He's a half-educated savage, and that makes him dangerous as hell."

Connors looked over toward me. "But I just told you, old chap. Canberra would never allow it."

"You're allowed a certain amount of discretion in emergencies, aren't you?" I suggested.

"Yes, but—"

"Declare yourself an emergency here in this district, and be slow in getting that word to Port Moresby. Have the wire sent after you've left for the interior with your troops."

"Don't tell them what I'm doing?" Connors said.

"Not until it's too late to do anything to stop you," I replied evenly.

Connors sat there staring at his cigarette. "I think I see how you get into so much trouble, Rainey. And I might go along with your thinking. But I have only thirty men here at Kikori. I could take maybe fifteen or twenty upriver with me. Kokoda has an armed army up there."

"My idea was not to challenge Kokoda with twenty colonial troops," I explained patiently, grimacing in pain when I moved my right arm. "You and I would go upriver with a cargo of our own guns, Connors. We would go to Merah, gather all his people from the entire area around him, and arm the best of them with your Smith & Wesson 9 mm carbines, and maybe some grenades. Then we'd have it out with Kokoda."

"A tribal war with modern weapons?" Connors said incredulously. "But that's just what we're trying to avoid, Rainey!"

"You're trying to avoid a one-sided slaughter by the Kiwais," I reminded him. "And this would not just be a tribal war. We would be running it. If we were lucky enough to win it, we would take our guns back from Merah and the Kiwais would be disarmed forcibly, and it would all be over."

Averill Connors stroked his square chin and regarded me balefully with the translucent eyes, his ruddy face very somber. But he was giving it a good think.

"You might end up a hero in Canberra," I added, "if you put Kokoda down before he arrives with his guns in Kikori. Can you imagine what he would do to the white men there, if he got this far?"

"I don't know," Connors muttered. "He does have respect for some of us, seemingly. It would depend on his whim, I suppose."

"Exactly," I agreed. "Is that the way you want it to be?"

Connors shook his head. "Of course not."

"We could take a dozen of your best men, and be ready to leave in a couple of days," I said. "And in the meantime, maybe we could locate those suppliers of Ruyker who did a number on me before I left last time with Ardrey. If you end their activities here, you stop Ruyker."

Connors stared hard at me for a moment, then a sly grin inched onto his face. "You're telling me my business, Rainey. And doing a bloody good job of it, I might add. By God, I'll do it. But we'll have to keep it quiet."

I smiled. "It's for God and country, Major—for you. I'll need a salary. Can you find a couple of grand in your petty cash?"

Connors shook his head. "I was told you're very careful about payment. I can get it together, somehow. You're more than worth it, I'd guess. You'll have a temporary rank equal to mine, too, with the boys. Does that suit you?"

"It sounds like we'll get along fine," I said.

Over the next couple of days, Connors and I picked a dozen of his station troops who seemed the toughest for the kind of action they might see.

A few of them had been upriver on a number of occasions, and could speak a couple of dialects. There were eight coastal-tribe natives and a half-caste in the enlisted ranks, and two non-coms who were Aussies, and a lieutenant who was part Tolai, part Aussie, and had a little Dutch blood in him, who was named Slattery. They were all tough-looking, hard-bitten men we could probably count on when the going got rough, as it undoubtedly would. I gave them a cram course in guerrilla actions, in those couple of days, and they seemed to absorb it well. Also, in that time, we searched Kikori for one or both of the men who had admitted being gun suppliers of Ruyker. Since there were only a few places in town that rented rooms, it did not take long to check them out. By noon of the second day we were convinced that they had gone back to Port Moresby, scared off for the moment. But then the mixed-caste Slattery came to Connors and me aboard the *Papuan Princess* that second afternoon, where we were preparing the boat for another trip up the river, and said he had heard of two white men living at a place out of town a short distance upriver—men who owned a car.

Connors and I decided to check it out, and took a Land Rover up a bake-oven-hot, dusty river road to where the men were supposed to be living. When we got there, we found an old house almost hidden by jungle, off the road about twenty yards, and backing onto the river.

We got out, Connors and I, and took our hand guns out. Connors had suggested we bring a couple of our people, but I figured the fewer there were of us, the more likely we would catch them

The Aust. Army is is Past & Present Master of Guerilla Warfare.

by surprise, if they were there. We walked up a dirt drive to the one-story cottage, in the brutal heat of the sun. Flies buzzed in our ears, and there was a stench not unlike that of feces coming from the river behind the house. There was an Austin sedan parked on the shady side of the house, with its windows rolled down.

We made it to the tiny front porch without incident, and Connors tried to peer inside through a window in the door, but he could not see anything. He gave me a signal, stood back slightl}, and kicked out savagely at the door.

The door crashed inward, and Connors and I went storming in, guns out. As soon as we got inside, into a small foyer, a shot rang out from a doorway to a living room, and the slug just missed Connors' head, slamming into the wall beside him. He fell into a deep crouch and returned fire to a place that was hidden from my view, firing off three quick rounds. The house reverberated with the shots, and there was a yell from the living room. Connors had gotten his assailant. But a moment later, there was a crashing of glass as a second person went through a closed window.

"You follow up here," I said loudly to Connors, then I charged back out through the door.

Outside, the sound of a car starting broke the silence and I knew there had been at least two of them—probably the same two who had worked me over, on that dark night in the hotel lobby.

I just got off the porch when the Austin came roaring into sight, squealing rubber on the gravel of the drive, heading for the road that paralleled the river. I knelt and held the Star with both hands, firing carefully at the head inside the car.

But the Austin swerved as I squeezed the trigger of the Star, and the shot caromed off metal instead of hitting my target. Now the car was putting distance between us. I fired once more, through the rear window, and just missed the head again, splintering glass in both the rear window and the windshield.

It was only ten paces to the Land Rover. I ran to it and threw myself into the vehicle bodily, turning the key in the ignition as soon as I hit the seat. The Rover roared to life, and I spun the wheels in a wild start after the Austin.

The gun runner in the other car had a hundred-yard lead on me when I hit the road in the Rover, and he immediately increased it from that in the first few seconds. But then I was pressing hard on the accelerator, making a great cloud of umber dust rise behind me as I raced down the road after him, eating his dirt. The distance was reduced to a hundred yards again, and then sixty. The road was rutted and bumpy, and I was thrown all over the front seat of the jeep-type Rover as I drove, fighting the wheel every yard of the way. I tried to hold the wheel with one hand and fire the Star with the other, but I hit a deep rut and almost lost control, going off toward a shallow ditch for a touchy moment, the Rover almost tipping over onto its side, then it came back and I controlled it.

I pulled up to within twenty yards of the Austin, and then ten, and when I got out to pass, I could see the gun runner's face, and he was the tall, tough-looking fellow of the twosome who had worked me over that night, the one who had done most of the kicking at my body and head, at the end. His long, bony face turned to me darkly, and then back to the road. I came up alongside, and twisted the wheel hard and crashed loudly into the side of the Austin.

The Austin went careening to the side of the road, slipping and sliding crazily for a moment, its door and quarter-panel dented deeply, and the rear wheel cover gone. But the gun runner got control and brought the car back onto the road surface. A moment later a Smith & Wesson revolver came swinging up to window level, and exploded toward me. The slug came into the open Rover and chipped at metal near my face, on the windshield frame. I hit another hole and swerved badly, almost going off the road, and dropping back on him again. On either side of the road now were deep ditches, with thick jungle on our left and marshy fields on the right. I fought for control and regained it, but the Austin had gained ground on me now. I wanted very much not to lose that bastard, after what he had done to me that night. I tried once more with the Star, this time letting up on the accelerator and letting the Austin gain a little more ground. I aimed past the windshield with my left hand, and fired off two quick shots toward the front wheel of the Austin, foregoing another shot at the driver.

On the second shot, the left front tire of the Austin exploded audibly above the roar of the engines, and the other vehicle began swerving violently from one side of the road to the other. I could see the gun runner wrestling with the wheel, but he was losing. In a moment the Austin swerved badly and went flying off the right side of the road bed, out into the ditch. I wheeled hard to miss going with it, then skidded to a slipping, sliding stop thirty yards beyond, kicking up a hot, white fog of dust in the blistering sun. The Austin had crashed hard in the ditch, then kept on going into the marshy field, bouncing hard. It finally rolled over twice in the muck, and crashed up against a young tree loudly, stopping there with a resounding rupture of metal and glass.

I got out of the Rover and walked down the ditch, jumping some muddy water at its bottom, then sloshed across the field carefully. When I got within ten yards I saw the tall man clearly, and he was no longer any danger to me or anybody. The car was partly on its side, and the tall man was hanging out its door. His right arm was hanging in a twisted, bent position, with an end of jagged, white bone protruding through the flesh, and the revolver was still clutched tightly in that hand. His face was crimson-smeared and the left side of it was crushed inward so that the features were gone there, and the left ear hung down on the neck. His glazed-over right eye told me he was very dead.

I holstered the Star. It appeared that Ruyker's source of weapons supplies had just dried up, in Kikori.

Now there was Ruyker, himself.

And the Kiwais.

SIX

Burke Ardrey had had no relatives or known heirs in Kikori or Port Moresby. He had been the kind of man who had cut his family ties as a young man, and then forgot them. Ardrey had been a true loner, and he had been satisfied with the life he had made for himself on New Guinea's rivers. Thinking back on it, I was certain that he would not have complained about the way he had died. He would have considered it as good a way to go as any. As for his head decorating Kokoda's trophy pole, Ardrey would have appreciated the ostentatious spectacle of it, even if he had chosen a few ear-burning Anglo-Saxon words to assail Kokoda with.

The *Papuan Princess*, in the absence of known beneficiaries of Ardrey's estate, had become an orphan. So Averill Connors merely confiscated the rusty old tub while he waited to hear from Canberra as to what its official disposition ought to be, and we left the very next morning for the interior.

Connors had only wounded the other gun runner, so that fellow was now in Connors' stockade, waiting to be transported to Port Moresby for arraignment and trial on a number of charges, and

Connors had sent a wire off, asking authorities there to find some way to put the bosses of these men there out of business. Connors figured he already had Ruyker nailed with attempted murder and other charges, if he chose to show his face in Kikori again.

The *Princess* was loaded down with cargo on our new trip upriver—both human and otherwise. We had brought our dozen guerrilla troops with their weapons—Sten Mark V submachine guns, two old mortars, grenades—and several crates of the S&W carbines and ammo for them. There was no place aboard for all of us to sleep—we also kept on Ardrey's remaining crew—but that did not matter, because we were not going to Bik Pella Post this time. The Bamu chief Merah had moved his headquarters south to make it harder for Kokoda to raid it, so we were taking a more southerly route into the jungle from the river. We were stopping at a small village called Ambo Kandam, a rather civilized trading village right on the river, and we hoped to be there by late afternoon.

The trip upriver was uneventful, and our few troops spent their time cleaning weaponry and getting their ammo rations. Connors and I sat in the sleazy cabin of the *Princess*, where Ardrey had conferred with us on that first night of our acquaintance, and discussed our route into the jungle. We would pass through some relatively unexplored territory to get to the Bamus this time, going by the most direct route. But Connors did not foresee that that would cause us any difficulty, except for the ruggedness of the terrain.

Connors' guess about the length of our river trip was pretty accurate, and we arrived at Ambo Kandam at just after 6:00 p.m. by Lieutenant Slattery's wrist watch. Ambo Kandam was bigger than Bik Pella Post, with a village square surrounded by several frame buildings. There were the usual chickens and dogs and naked children, but the adults wore lap-laps of store-bought cloth there, and none of them wore nose or ear decorations. They considered themselves as civilized as the town-dwellers of Kikori, and welcomed us to make camp in the public square that night. We did, sleeping out under the stars on the ground, on bedrolls. The men were accustomed to such outings, and were quite comfortable. Slattery and the two Aussie non-coms—a couple of toughs named Jenkins and Boggs—volunteered to do night watch in shifts, so the rest of us rested secure. When morning came I was a little stiff from the hard dirt of the compound, but felt better than I had in days.

We were off at dawn. Connors took up the scouting position with a rather wild-looking private, and I brought up the rear of the column. The foot march was much like that I made with Ardrey previously, except that we left the trail shortly after we cleared Ambo Kandam, and headed right into the thick of the jungle. Every man had a machete, and the fore-runners had to use them. Lianas and creepers grabbed at our legs and arms, entwining around us, and thickets of bamboo forced us to make wide detours. By mid-morning sweat was sticking my shirt to my back, and the heat was becoming a physical weight on my shoulders.

At noon we took a much-deserved break, just as I was beginning to think Connors would never stop. Connors did not look all that tough, but he was. He had stamina that is rare in a white man. His native troops who followed him through that jungle showed their exhaustion before he did. I think he took a certain pride in that. He was grinning widely when I dropped down beside him at break time, in an open forest glade surrounded by high trees.

"You looked a bit weary, old boy. I thought I'd stop a bit early and give you a rest."

Sweat ran down my face and I wiped briefly at it, gasping for oxygen in the wet heat. "I could have gone a lot further," I remarked sourly. "With two of your best men carrying me."

Connors grinned and removed his Aussie-type wide-brimmed hat. We were all wearing them, and the fatigue-green uniform. Every man also carried a Sten Mark V on a sling, and Connors, Slattery and I wore pistols on our hips. Mine was the stubby Star .45 that I had lost temporarily to Kokoda.

The dark-skinned Slattery came up and squatted down beside Connors and me. The two noncoms lay red-faced against the base of a tree nearby. Slattery pushed his hat back off his forehead, showing his dark, glittery eyes. He was an intelligent half-breed, with an ambitious drive inside him that made him a good and dependable officer.

"We're within a hour's march of the isolated Sepik village," Slattery said in his deep voice. "Are we going to detour it?"

Connors nodded. "Rainey might get a kick out of meeting them, but we couldn't get out of there without a delay. They would expect a several-hour visit."

"What's so special about them?" I asked wearily.

Connors turned to me. "They're the famous airstrip-watchers," he told me. "Have you heard of them?"

"I don't believe so," I said, slapping at a persistent mosquito.

Slattery grunted. "The poor, bloody fools. They worship at an abandoned air field, watching for the return of a plane that will never come."

Connors continued the story. "We had an air supply field out here during the war with the Japs, and for a while afterward. Transport planes landed right adjacent to their village for a couple of years, and brought white men who handed out food and trinkets occasionally to them. Then suddenly the planes—which they considered great silver birds—did not come anymore. They watched and waited, searching the sky in vain. Slowly, a religion developed from the waiting, and the god was the silver bird that never returned, but that they are certain will, some day. So they keep a constant vigil, even today, at the perimeter of the airstrip, praying to a silver-winged god that lies rusting in some scrap metal yard in Port Moresby. It's all a bit depressing, really."

"And nobody has tried to explain it to them?" I suggested.

"Oh, yes. But they believed what they wished. Nobody tries to discredit their god now. It's become too ingrained a part of them, of what they are."

I shook my head. "I think I'd believe almost anything about the inhabitants of this green wasteland now," I said. "I don't think I've ever encountered such—"

Slattery touched my arm with his hand. "Major Rainey. Please don't move."

I met his eyes curiously, then glanced down at the long trass beside me. A bright green snake had slithered out into the open just a few inches from my left leg, and was watching me warily. I froze in position, holding my breath.

Connors saw the reptile, too. "Pay attention to Slattery, old man," he said slowly and deliberately.

I was not about to do otherwise. Slattery reached to his machete on his hip, and drew it out in a gentle, liquid motion. The snake was still watching me, trying to decide whether I was a threat to it, and had not seen Slattery's movement. A tense muscle jerked my arm involuntarily, just a fractional inch, and the snake coiled and prepared to strike. Slattery raised the machete and swung it downward in a quick, precise up-down motion.

The snake's head jumped off its body as the machete thumped into the ground under it, and the body of the snake writhed and twisted beside me, already dead.

I breathed again. "Goddam!" I muttered.

"One small bite, Major," Slattery told me, wiping the edge of the blade on his trousers, "and we'd have had to bury you here."

"The poison takes as little as thirty seconds to wor," Connors added gravely. "You were very lucky, Rainey, to have Slattery around."

"Thanks," I said to the bronze-skinned officer. I rose from the grass tensely. "I'm ready to get out of here any time you people are."

Connors grinned the amiable grin. "Okay, Rainey. I think I see your point."

We marched single file through that steaming jungle for three more hours after wolfing down a standing-up lunch at the snake site. In mid-afternoon Slattery spotted smoke rising above the trees, just off to our right, in a very mountainous region. He and Connors and I conferred under a wild fruit tree, and Connors decided he had never seen a village in this area before.

"Maybe they're Bamus," he suggested, "and can tell us where to find Merah's new headquarters. Let's have a look."

"Good," I said. "I could use another break."

In twenty minutes our column had inched down a hillside, hacking our way every yard, and climbed up the steep side of the next green hump in the jungle. The village sat on a flat area on top of the hill.

It was a small, primitive village, and not one native was visible when we first arrived in its clearing. Connors looked all around, and made an announcement.

"I don't believe this place is noted on the maps," he said.

"I agree, Major Connors," Slattery said.

The non-com called Boggs, a squatty, wiry fellow with a jutting jaw and gunmetal-gray eyes, came up beside us. "There's a look to them what ain't never seen a white man, Major, and this place has got it."

"Boggs is certain right this time," the taller, hard-bitten Jenkins said from behind me.

Connors nodded. "Maybe." He called one of his native privates up to him, and the fellow came running with his Sten gun. Connors took the gun from him. "Now go on in to the center of the village, and find out if we're welcome."

The soldier nodded, and walked on up past the first huts. They were just lean-tos, with thatch roofs and sides. A fire glowed in a central open area. The soldier stood near the fire and called out in a dialect I had never heard before. In a moment, a short, wiry aborigine came tentatively from a hut, and then another. The soldier spoke to them, and they did not act as if they understood. In just moments, there were a couple dozen men out in sight, staring toward us with dark, distrustful faces. They wore small skins on their loins, and polished-stone necklaces, and long, sharp bones through their very flat, wide noses. Their bloodshot eyes had the look of hunted animals. They kept their distance from the soldier, even though he was unarmed, and most of them kept staring very hard at the rest of us in our strange costumes and gear. Most of them could not take their eyes off Connors and me and the two Aussie non-coms, with our pale skins. We went on into the village cautiously now, the fourteen of us, and Connors put his native troops up front. More men came from the twenty-or-so huts, but we only got glimpses of women, peering out from dark doorways. Connors stepped toward one of the larger men—a fellow who did not come much above Connors' shoulder in height—and the fellow unashamedly shrank back, stumbling backwards a couple of steps. This caused some dark mutterings from the rest of them, and more suspicious looks.

"We intend you no harm," Connors said to the foremost man. "We come to you in peace." He took a hand mirror from a tunic pocket, and showed it to the fellow, offering it to him.

The aborigine shrank back another step, then looked in fascination at the shiny object. "There's no doubt of it," Connors told me quietly, watching him. "These people have never laid eyes on a white man before. We must look like bloody Martians to them. Look at the fear in their faces, Rainey."

"If we relax, maybe they will," I said.

"I agree," Slattery said, from behind me. "You fellows there. Get those guns on your backs, and out of sight."

A few of the native troops slid the Sten guns around further onto their backs. Connors offered the mirror again, speaking Bamu this time. The aborigine, encouraged by a couple of his comrades, took the mirror gingerly.

As we all watched, the nearest men to him gathered around him as he peered at the mirror. When he spied his own face there, his mouth dropped open and his eyes saucered in shock. He muttered something to his comrades, and they all took a look. In just minutes, they were jabbering excitedly, passing the mirror from one to another, the looks on their faces a study in primitive human behavior. There was surprise and fear, but there was also courage. It was all a very serious business to them.

"If I hear one muffled laugh," Connors said pleasantly to his men, "there'll be a bloody court-martial, you can count on it."

The villagers relaxed some after the mirror had been passed around, and then they all gathered closer to our four white faces, studying them with frank interest. Connors found one of the younger ones who understood a dialect known by a native private, and they got into a lengthy conversation while Connors entertained the other men with his wallet and a ring of keys.

"Imagine their reaction to a radio," he suggested to me, while they examined his personal property.

"Or to one of these guns going off," I added. "God, Kokoda would make mince-meat of people like this."

"He will, if he isn't stopped," Connors said. He turned as the aborigine soldier came up to him, the fellow who had been speaking with the local.

"What did you find out, Private?" Connors asked.

"This fellow he say Bamu village very close, maybe two-three mile in that direction." He pointed off toward the northeast, through the thick jungle. "Bamus make new village there. These afraid, they know Bamus headhunters."

"The Bamus also have guns now, thanks to Ruyker," I commented.

"Yes," Connors said bleakly. "Well, let's leave these people some food and mirrors and such, and see if they have any water for us, and then press on," he told the rest of us. "We have two or three hours of light left. If the going isn't too bad, we ought to be able to get there before dark."

Slattery nodded. "Jenkins, Boggs! Prepare the men to move out!"

In fifteen minutes we were ready to leave, with most of the villagers staring hard at us, numb with the shock of it all. Just as we were preparing to go, the fellow who had first peered into the mirror

—he appeared to be their chief—came from a hut carrying something tentatively. Connors saw him approach us first, and nudged me. I turned and regarded the fellow incredulously as he stopped before us. He was carrying a freshly-decapitated child, a mere baby, in his hands.

"Good God," I muttered.

"He's just killed it," Connors said quietly.

Slattery, Jenkins and Boggs all stared blankly at the fellow as he offered the butchered child to me personally. The other troops came around us slowly. The baby's corpse was still letting a lot of blood onto the ground, and it was all very messy.

"I think—I understand," Slattery said numbly. He asked the private to translate what the local was telling me and Connors now, and there was a round of translation, and Slattery turned back to us.

"This is his first-born son, who he has just killed. He believes we are cannibals, and offers this sacrifice to us so that we will go in peace and think well of his people."

I stood there dumbfounded. Now we could hear the mother in a nearby hut, wailing softly in there. It was all very unbelievable to me.

"Let's get to hell out of here, Connors," I told him.

But to my surprise, Connors stepped forward and held out his arms to receive the small, dark corpse. The local gave it to him, and Connors thanked him in a dialect, and then turned to me.

"Smile and thank him," he said. "If we reject his offer, he will lose too much face, and will lose his position in the tribe—probably even be murdered by the other men."

"But good God, Connors—" I protested.

"Be a good chap, Rainey," Connors insisted.

I sighed heavily, then smiled a stiff smile at the father of the dead baby, thanking him. He grinned, and there seemed to be a slight relaxation among the locals. Slattery gave the corpse over to a private, and we moved off then with it wrapped in a piece of mosquito netting, moving off into the jungle again. When we got deep into the forest, about halfway to the Bamu village, we took a ten minute break and gave the infant a burial under a big tree.

Our chance discovery of those most primitive of peoples had cost them a life—one that had just started. I wondered how a thousand mirrors and trinkets could ever make up to them for that loss, and for the loss of security and dignity they had encountered for the first time in such a traumatic way.

It was just possible they would never be quite the same, after that brief exposure to severe culture shock.

It now seemed more important than ever to save this kind of Cro-Magnon innocence from the effects of Ruyker's upriver trading.

We arrived at the new Bamu village on hour before sunset, with plenty of light still in the sky. The village sat on a high, level table of hard ground between two green peaks, and every hut there was new. But, unfortunately, the Kiwais had already found the new site, and had made a raid on it while Merah and his people were still reorganizing. We found out later that that had occurred just hours before our arrival.

It was ugly.

There were still corpses lying around in the clearing, and huts were burning, the black smoke curling thick into a yellow sky. Women sat on the ground and wailed over dead husbands and children, some of whom had lost their heads. Men wandered about in a daze, inspecting what was left of their new village. They looked defeated now. They had finally had enough, you could see it in their faces.

When they saw our column straggle into the village, they all stopped what they were doing and stared somberly at us. The new community hut had escaped being burned, and Merah sat inside the open-sided structure, on a pallet on the ground, looking blankly at his village. I could see the priest Zigibi near him, standing rigidly at Merah's side, muttering some words into the silent air, and waving a baton about to ward off further evil.

Merah saw us as we halted in the village's center, and Connors put his troops at ease. He and I walked over to the big hut somberly, and went inside and joined Merah and Zigibi. Zigibi still considered us outsiders meddlings in their private affairs, so was no happier to see us than he had been on that previous occasion to welcome Ardrey and me at the other headquarters.

"Mr. Rainey!" Merah said in surprise. "I thought your head pretty-make Kokoda-pole. Much please, Major Connors."

"Good to see you, Merah," Connors told him. "What happened here?"

"Kiwais find Merah," the squatty, pot-bellied chief told us somberly. "Where we look-go now?

They take shoot-sticks, kill warriors, steal women. Bamu soon-become Kiwai."

What Merah said was true, if Connors and I could not turn the tables very quickly. The Bamus were beaten. We sat down near Merah on pallets, and Zigibi acknowledged our presence with a nod of his ugly head. When he was not wearing a ceremonial mask, he was almost more odd-looking than with it. His hair stuck out several inches from his head all around, and he wore an enormous sliver of bone in his nose, and a curved one in his lower lip. His face was decorated with permanent dyes in exotic patterns, and he wore a necklace and belt of bright feathers and shells. In his left earlobe was a small mirror, and in the right, a carved ornament. He had been wounded by a spear, in the left side, and blood was caked there now.

Merah was holding his right arm, and I saw it was gunshot, from one of the Volkssturm rifles. It looked bad, but he did not seem to pay any attention to it.

"The Bamu will remain Bamu, and the Kiwai must withdraw to their original territories," Connors said firmly, even though he was not all that sure we could stop Kokoda now. "Mr. Rainey, who is now Major Rainey of the Australian army, has agreed to return to help the Bamus and Merah. He is a great soldier from behind the wide waters and knows much of war-with-guns."

Merah regarded me closely. I turned and yelled at Jenkins, who stood outside the hut. "Bring a case of the carbines in, Jenkins."

"Yes, sir, Major, sir," Jenkins replied.

I turned back to Merah. "We come with weapons even greater than those of Kokoda," I told him. "Guns that shoot better and faster. And grenades that make big explosions and kill many at once and two large guns."

"And Major Rainey has the knowledge about them necessary to teach your warriors how to use them efficiently," Connors said, in Bamu, as two men now came into the hut with the opened crate of carbines.

Merah looked at the crate with great interest as I took a Smith & Wesson 9 mm carbine from the container and worked the cocking mechanism briefly and then handed it to him. He took it and turned it over in his hands with an ill-concealed fondness. Zigibi leaned over his shoulder, his dark eyes glittery with new excitement.

Merah was talking now in Bamu, and Connors translated for me. Merah was saying that the guns were beautiful indeed, and he was very pleased that we had come to save his people from the Kiwai. But, he told us, his people close around him were much reduced in strength and no match for the small army that Kokoda was building.

"We know that," I said. "But what we're going to do, Merah, is go out in this wide territory and bring in all Bamus we find in it, and gather them here at this new headquarters village. There must be hundreds left, scattered in villages and communal sites."

Merah understood most of that, and nodded, and rattled off some fast Bamu. Connors turned to me. "He says there are many Bamus left, if we could get them all together. But that that would be a very large job."

"A job," I said to Merah, "that must be accomplished, for survival. We have the men to do it, and it should be accomplished in just a few days, if we're to be ready for Kokoda's next big attack. You'll pick some men who know the locations of all the other Bamu villages and sites, and send them out as your couriers with the urgent message that we must unite to survive. And I'll begin training a dozen of your very best and smartest warriors to use these carbines, and about military strategy."

Connors had to translate that time, and even then I was not sure Merah understood. There was some more discussion about arms and training, and then darkness fell and we settled our troops in. Merah had agreed to our plan, but I was not sure he believed in it.

I was not even certain that I did.

In the next few days, though, hundreds of Bamus began pouring into the new village that we were rebuilding. It was amazing to watch. All through the days and nights they straggled in, from whole villages of close to a hundred to single family units. The response to our plea for unity was overwhelming. Almost all of them had been harassed or terrorized by Kokoda's marauding Kiwais, and knew well that safety—if there was safety—lay in cohesion. There were several lesser chieftains who had more or less pledged loyalty to Merah, but who now were faced with relegation to mere lieutenants with their own people for the first time ever. Surprisingly, there were few difficulties. The presence of the white man in their midst, and our recognition of Merah as the big chief, was the additional cohesive factor they needed for real unity, it seemed.

In that short week we organized the new, united Bamus into a social and military unit, and began training them for modern warfare. Slattery and the non-coms and several of the more experienced privates worked hard under Connors and me, and slowly the Bamu savages learned how to fire guns, and aim them at people. It was not a happy undertaking. It would have been far better if they had not ever had to learn about firearms. But Ruyker's intrusion into their world, and Kokoda's readiness to accept him, had put us all beyond that. Now guns had become temporarily necessary to physical survival, and that had top prioity.

Also during those few days we were obliged to stand guard duty, and make routine patrols out into the jungle, to make sure Kokoda had not found out about our efforts and was planning to sabotage them with an all-out attack. We took turns on these patrols, and on the fourth day I led a four-man patrol in a wide sweep of the mountainous jungle around us.

We left in mid-afternoon, and it was like taking a hot shower, going into that steaming jungle. I was on point in our strung-out patrol, with the Star on my hip, a Sten Mark V slung on my shoulder, and a machete to hack my way through the thick places. It was rough going, if you did not stick to the trails, and I was trained not to. That was the way to end up dead. We must have hiked for over two hours and were heading back toward the village headquarters, when we got our big surprise.

I heard the familiar crack of a rifle nearby, from foliage, and a branch of a tree splintered beside my head, missing killing me by a half-inch.

A second shot rang out almost immediately, and the native private behind me choked out a yell and the side of his head disintegrated. He hit a thicket and fell onto his side, his left leg kicking violently.

"*Down! Take cover!*" I yelled out.

Now there was rifle fire all around us, the slugs chipping into trees and shaking shrubbery. A second trooper screamed, groin-shot, and threw his Sten gun to the ground. He did a small pirouette and fell onto his back, clutching at a bloody place at his crotch.

I was sure that the Kiwais had found us, because I recognized the reports of the rifles as Volkssturms. But then I saw a familiar head poke out from a tree through the foliage, and recognized Hendrik Ruyker.

"*I told you not to follow me, Rainey!*" he was now yelling.

I swore under my breath, then yelled back. "*You stupid Dutchman, Ruyker! We're not here for you! You're killing for nothing, damn you!*"

"*You're finished this time, Rainey! You're on my killing ground!*"

My people were returning fire now, and I heard one of Ruyker's armed porters yell and go down. I figured there must be eight of them, including Ruyker. Another of Ruyker's people yelled out, from behind foliage.

"*Use those damned guns!*" I yelled at my two last men. They had been shooting just short bursts.

Now the three of us began raking the foliage with the Sten submachine guns, the weapons making a dinning, clattering racket in the jungle, pounding the trees all around. I saw Ruyker poke his head out in surprise now, because he had not expected automatic fire. I kept the trigger pressed back hard, and the Sten gun banged out savagely, raking the foliage with hot lead, the weapon sweat-slippery in my hands. Two more of Ruyker's men yelled, and then another one. We did not have to visually locate them, with the Stens. My two people understood that now, and were firing heavily into the underbrush. There was another yell, and then I saw a Ruyker native break for better cover. I followed him with a hail of lead, and hit him in the arm, back and head. He jerked in mid-stride, over and over again, and then disappeared into the high brush.

"Damn you, Rainey!" I heard Ruyker yell now. *"It's not over between us!"* I heard him giving orders to his people, then, to withdraw, and I got a glimpse again of his scarred, long face as he turned and retreated to the cover of a big tree. I fired after him, but did not get him.

A moment later, our opposition was magically gone. The trooper who had been groin-shot had quit yelling, and had died, so there was a sudden unnerving silence around us again. I glanced around and saw that my other two soldiers were unhurt.

"Good shooting," I told them. "Let's see what damage we did."

The three of us moved through the thickets slowly then. But Ruyker was really gone. In several minutes of searching we found out what he had left behind—five dead. They were really raked over, most of them. There were bloody holes in arms, legs, torsos. One of them had been hit seven times, once in the face. Another had had a leg almost severed by two closely-targeted slugs. There was a lot of blood. The Stens had proved their worth against Ruyker's—and Kokoda's—VK-98's.

The trouble was, Ruyker was gone again, and so was the cargo of arms he had undoubtedly been carrying with him. He was still free to continue his death-dealing in the jungle.

And his biggest customer was out after our heads.

SEVEN

Averill Connors was shocked when we limped back into the village less two of his troops. I don't think he had really expected to lose any. One of the men who were killed had been with Connors at Kikori ever since Connors had arrived there, several years ago.

As for Merah, he did not understand why we did not try to buy more guns from Ruyker, in that jungle meeting. I had explained that the S&W rifles were not enough to arm all the warriors we were collecting around us, and Merah wanted them all armed. But I knew that most of them would never be able to learn enough about firearms to ever be effective with a gun.

A group of Bamu warriors went out to recover the bodies of Ruyker's dead, against Connors' objections. He knew what they wanted with them. He finally talked Merah into letting him send Slattery along, to make sure nothing happened to the bodies of his two soldiers. Slattery buried them out there where the firefight had taken place. When Merah's warriors returned, they had five decapitated heads with them, all from Ruyker's armed porters, and a couple of bloody thighs. Merah was jubilant, and the heads went up on trophy poles around the enlarged village, and this seemed to give the newcomers—there were several hundred now—a feeling of unity. Connors allowed that, but insisted that Merah give up on preparing a feast with the thighs cut off the Ruyker dead. Those bloody parts were finally buried just outside the burgeoning village.

Wherever we turned in the new Bamu headquarters in those next couple of days, we would see those grisly heads staring down at us, and it was a grim reminder that Merah and his Bamus were not all that different from Kokoda and his bloodthirsty Kiwais. The difference was mostly in leadership, and perhaps in opportunity. These were, after all, savages we were arming for this hopefully temporary war, and we had to go carefully.

The new village now sprawled over an area several hundred yards across. Connors and I had supervised the building of a second community hut centrally, where we and our troops slept and cooked for ourselves. Adjacent to the village we built a small firing range for training Merah's warriors with the S&W semi-automatic rifles. I have never seen such ineptness about firearms and things mechanical. In the first few days of training, three men were shot by accident—one fatally —and Slattery came close to getting his head blown off. I could not help but wonder whether they would kill more Kiwais than each other, when a battle came. The carbines, though light for a rifle, were pretty big and bulky for the slightly-built Bamus, and they had a hell of a time with them.

I figured on arming a hundred of them with the

carbine rifles, and keeping the two old mortars and the grenades in the hands of Connors' troops. We practiced with the mortars and grenades in those days, too, and the Bamus were scared to death by both. I did not blame them. They were fearful weapons to a primitive people. I hoped they might make some difference against Kokoda, because he probably had twice the rifles that we had, even though they were semi-automatic guns. I also hoped that the Sten guns Connors' troops would use would help make up the difference in firepower.

Lastly, I hoped Kokoda would not realize just how superior our weaponry was, until it was too late to defend against it. Ruyker was headed, indirectly, toward Kiwai territory again, I knew, and he had already gotten a good look at the Stens. He would find great pleasure in confiding our strength to Kokoda. It might even save his life. Ruyker was not really aware, I figured, just how angry Kokoda was with his double-dealing.

When we had been there just under a week, our little war in the jungle began.

Connors and I were sitting in our big open-sided hut, discussing how to make the Bamus understand just what ammunition was, in relation to the guns. They did not really believe, yet, that the bullet actually left the gun when it was fired. In the middle of that inane discussion, Merah came to us, his face wild with excitement. One of his warriors was with him, a man we had sent on patrol with Corporal Jenkins. Jenkins had sent the man back to the village as a runner, Merah now told us, to warn us of the approach of a large Kiwai raiding party.

Connors and I were both on our feet in a moment.

"Are you sure?" I asked.

Merah understood. "Yes, yes. No wrong-make, is Kiwai."

"How far away are they?" Connors asked him.

"Maybe one drumbeat, also-maybe more," Merah reported. "Not very-much far."

Connors turned to me. "He means they're within earshot of the log drums. That's a mile or two. We have a brief time for defense, it would seem." He turned back to Merah. "Where are the others? Jenkins and the lot?"

"They quick-come after look-see," Merah said. He had already questioned the Bamu warrior in his own language.

"Okay," I told Connors, sweating suddenly in the mid-afternoon heat. "We're lucky this time. Now we can see if we've learned anything."

"I'll get the trainees together," Connors said quickly. "Maybe we can trust some of them with carbines. And our people will have the Stens. We'll stop them outside the village with a mortar shot, then try to take the offensive."

I shook my head. "No, we can do better than that, Connors. I suspect this raiding party doesn't know about our guns yet, or they wouldn't be approaching us with such openness. That means we can really give them a surprise party."

Connors hesitated, then nodded. "All right, Rainey. I hired you to come out here because you know what you're doing. Issue your orders."

My respect for Connors grew even more in that moment. I thanked him, and turned to Merah and the others who had now gathered around us, including Slattery and Boggs.

"Move the women and children out! Now!" I said loudly to them.

Merah regarded me curiously. "We run again too-soon?"

"We do *not* run," I told him. "This time we fight. But we fight in such a way as to kill the most Kiwais."

A slow grin came onto his face. The priest Zigibi came up, and spoke animatedly to Merah, and Connors translated for me. "Our patrol is back," he said.

"Good. Evacuate the village immediately!" I said to them. "And then gather our warriors here centrally—I want only men who can fire a carbine. The others may go off to protect the women, in case they have any trouble. Let's move!"

The word spread quickly about the evacuation, and in minutes the women and children were being herded out of the village, in the opposite direction from the one where the Kiwais were coming. Most of the men went with them this time, too, because I wanted only firearms used in this action. When Jenkins and his men came running into the village clearing from the trees a few minutes later, the village was half-evacuated already. Connors and I met the dirt-streaked, sweating Jenkins in the village center, and he collapsed onto a big fire log.

"They're only ten minutes away," he gasped out. "There must be fifty Kiwais. Every bloody one's got a bloody rifle. They look mean, lads."

"Is Kokoda with them?" I asked.

He shook his head negatively. "We didn't see him."

"He wouldn't go on a raid, ordinarily," Connors told me. "He prefers the spectacle of open battle, on a pre-chosen battleground. With all the ritual and color."

"Well, maybe we can make him wish he hadn't missed this color," I suggested. "Slattery! Boggs! Get your squad leaders together! Put each trooper in charge of some armed Bamus! And station them all around the village, out in the thick stuff, in a horseshoe shape, leaving the northwest open for the Kiwais to enter our trap. Get them out far enough so they won't be seen, heard, or smelled. But close enough so that they can close in in seconds and open up with the carbines and Stens. Hide the mortars and grenades, we won't use them. Let's do it! Now!"

Merah and Zigibi watched dumbfounded as our new little army began reacting to my orders. They had never seen any such order and efficiency. They insisted on staying and defending the village with the armed men, despite Merah's busted-up arm and Zigibi's wound, so I let them go with Slattery and his group. Connors was going to control one leg of the horseshoe-shaped trap, and I the other.

In just a few more minutes the village was deserted. The women and children were now a half-mile or more off in the jungle, and the gun-carrying warriors were situating themselves in a tight but open-ended ring around the village, well out of sight, according to my orders. Connors and I were the last to leave, and I took a good look around. There were two fires still burning, and everything looked very peaceful. That was the way I wanted it.

We were under an order of silence now. I motioned to Connors, and he nodded. We left the village together. We moved out to a position between the feet of the horseshoe, and then separated, taking up our positions with our men.

I had several Bamus strung out between me and the next squad leader, Boggs. They crouched now behind trees and deep in the underbrush and waited, their faces full of fear. After a short time we heard the movements in the jungle, and then they came.

They appeared one at a time along a short front, making their way as quietly as possible through the trees. They were heading right into the open end of our horseshoe. They were some of Kokoda's wildest-looking warriors, with bones in their noses, and wild, bushy hair and paint on their faces and bodies. Each and every man carried a VK-98 rifle, one of the guns I had sold Ruyker back in Sydney. They were well supplied.

We crouched deep in the undergrowth, and watched and waited. One by one they passed by, moving up on to the perimeter of the Bamu village carefully, gesturing to each other occasionally. In a few minutes they were all within the horseshoe, and the estimate had been right. There were almost fifty of them. Enough to slaughter the remnants of a village Merah had had there when Connors and I arrived.

There were about the same numbers of us, but there would be a difference beyond that. This time we had the better weapons, and we also had the element of surprise. I watched as the first of the Kiwais motioned back to the others, and then they started yelling and screaming as they stormed into the village.

We immediately moved in to close the horseshoe into a circle. There was some scattered shooting by the Kiwais as they entered the village, and then it tapered off as they began to realize the place was deserted. They must have also been surprised by its much larger size than they had expected. Now, as we closed the circle on them, they were rushing into huts with their rifles, trying to find somebody to shoot.

We came up close now, and the village was in clear view. Connors was off to my left, and I glanced toward him and nodded. I could see a movement of brush at the opposite end of the village, and then another. Our people were in place. But I waited. The Kiwais came out of the huts slowly, and began congregating in the open center of the village. I waited some more, until almost all of them were out there and visible. Then I raised my hand in the air and dropped it abruptly.

Connors' group and mine opened up with the Stens and carbines, and that was the signal for the rest of them. In the next instant the jungle was filled with the banging and clattering of gunfire, with hot lead raining into the village like a thunderstorm.

The Kiwais were caught flat-footed in that hail of lead, and began yelling and going down. In the first few seconds about a third of them were hit with the devastating, raking fire. Skulls exploded and chests and backs were punched with hot slugs and bones were shattered. After that initial shock, they began yelling and running and returning fire. But we were still well-hidden and they were hitting nothing. A few of them tried to get out of it, and ran from one group of guns into the teeth of others. It was murderous, and it was deadly. The

Stens burped out their message over and over, spitting up streams of lead that tore flesh and mashed bone and tore the enemy to pieces. A couple of the Kiwais became so afraid that they threw the Volkssturms down and just tried to find a place to hide. But there was none.

"All right!" I finally yelled. *"Go in and get the rest of them!"*

Connors and Slattery and a couple of Connors' privates yelled out the command in Bamu, and then we rushed into the village. We went in there like howling demons, and I did not try to hold down the emotion. The Bamus were entitled, and so were we. Merah and Zigibi rushed in from the left flank with carbines firing fast but wild, and now we were all inside the village. A few Kiwais had hidden among the new huts, and they fired desperately as they were sought out. One of them killed Jenkins with one lucky hit to the center chest, and two more of Connors' troopers went down, hit badly. But in just moments the Kiwai were swarmed over, shot up, and killed vengefully. One wounded Kiwai managed to escape to the edge of the village, and a trooper started after him.

"No!" I yelled. *"Let him go! Let him go tell Kokoda what happened here!"*

The trooper returned, and the Kiwai disappeared into the jungle.

I turned then and stood in the hot sun and surveyed the carnage. It was pretty ugly. It was perhaps the most effective massacre I had ever been a part of. Kiwais lay all around the village, in twisted, awkward positions of death. Even more so than with Ruyker's porters, they were literally ripped to pieces by hot lead. Blood soaked into the ground and lay in pools around them. Flesh was chewed up by the high-velocity slugs from the Stens and carbines.

Connors came over to me, looking weary and dirty. His Sten gun hung on his broad shoulder. "Well, Rainey. You did it, by God. You gave Kokoda something to think about."

"I hope so," I said heavily. "I suspect, though, that this may just whet his appetite." I looked across the compound, where Merah was encouraging two of his warriors in the beheading of several Kiwais near them.

"Maybe," I added pensively, "it will whet Merah's, too." I knew that at some point, if we managed to disarm Kokoda, we would also have to take the carbines back from Merah, and convince him that vengeance had to end somewhere.

Connors nodded. "Let's hope to God we haven't started something we can't finish," he said quietly.

EIGHT

There was a big, formal celebration that evening in the Bamu village, and Kiwai heads decorated newly-hewn trophy poles all over the perimeter. It was all very Pleistocene. It was like going back in a time machine for about a million years. There was dancing and weird chanting and drumming, and Merah allowed the butchery and roasting of a Kiwai corpse, despite Connors' objections. Our army guerrillas stayed apart, in our own shelter, partaking of provisions we had brought from Kikori.

Merah was a different man. He took on a regal bearing again now, and seemed more like Motu Kokoda than I would have imagined. He made it clear that these were his people we had surrounded him with, and that it was he, Merah, that was their leader—not Connors or I. He was already talking about a big attack on the nearest Kiwai village, which would be a complete devastation, and in which they would bring back many heads, and young maidens as slaves.

The high priest Zigibi reveled in his chief's refound pride, resuming his arrogant manner toward us. He figured that they no longer needed us, I guessed, and was probably filling Merah's head with those ideas.

The following morning brought a surprise. A routine patrol of ours ran into a Kiwai runner from Kokoda, carrying a truce sign, and he brought the message that Kokoda wished to palaver with Connors and me that afternoon, on neutral ground between our headquarters and his northern one. He made no mention of bringing Merah.

Connors and I had not expected this kind of thing, and it raised our hopes that Kokoda was frightened by our armed might, and wanted to talk peace. But such was not to be the case.

At shortly after noon we left for the site described by Kokoda, with some trepidation. We were taking only Slattery, a private soldier, and Merah. Kokoda had said we might not bring more than three others, and we did not want to ruin a possible chance for peace talks by doing otherwise. But I could not help but worry that Kokoda was setting a trap to get rid of the Bamu leadership, which he considered to be Connors and myself.

When we arrived at the jungle stream where Kokoda said he would meet us, however, he was there with just three warriors and his priest Titimua, just as he had promised. At least, there was no evidence that he had any armed men hiding in the trees nearby. We met on an open meadow beside the bank of the stream, with high, green hills all around us. It was a pristine setting, and a memorable one. Kokoda appeared angry for a moment, when he spotted Merah, but then the two of them exchanged formal greetings in a very dignified manner, and we all sat down on a straw mat to smoke those asphyxiating pipes for a while before getting down to business. Kokoda, Merah, Titimua, Connors and I formed a loose circle on the ground, while our armed people stood nearby glaring at each other.

Kokoda looked very royal, despite his primitive appearance. Next to Merah, he looked, also, very physical. I had the idea that he could very well fight his own battles. He was bigger than anybody there except for Connors, Slattery and me, and his wiry muscles had muscles. When he saw that we wanted Merah included in the talks, he was quite polite to Merah.

"It is pleasant to see you again, Rainey," he said in his deep, hollow voice. "Even though you come with the blood of Kiwais on your hands."

I ignored the challenge. "It is good, rich blood," I said.

"I should have killed you without ceremony, when I had you in my power," he grinned broadly.

"Yes," I said, "you should have."

He turned to Connors. "And what a distinct honor to meet with the Major again. Surely you have enough business in Kikori to keep you busy, Major, without chasing savages through the forest. It is beneath your station."

Connors grunted. "Tell them that in Canberra."

"I did not know that you had joined Rainey and the honorable Merah against the Kiwai, Major Connors," Kokoda went on.

Merah spoke up now. "Bamu he be too-much good-fellow with bik pella chiefs in white-man Kikori, no go-around cut bik pella law with gun."

Kokoda regarded Merah diffidently. "What you know about white man, Merah? I live with them many years, speak their language." His English became simpler, to accommodate Merah's lack of understanding of it. "Kiwai is for Kiwai, Bamu for Bamu, bik pella government for white man." Bik pella was a name used to describe the Australian government in Port Moresby, by the aborigine.

The ugly Titimua nodded his head in agreement, understanding most of what Kikoda had said. "Is same," he added in a gravelly hard voice.

I remembered how Titimua had stood before me and announced my very slow demise, in that Kiwai village. It was no wonder the Kiwais and Bamus had been at each other's throats for centuries, I figured, with advisors like Titimua and Zigibi around.

Connors spoke up again. "The bik pella government was formed to protect the mighty aborigine in the jungle," he said. "I do not take sides in your battles, Kokoda. But when modern weapons are introduced into a primitive world by a white man, it is the white man's responsibility to correct the situation. We cannot have Kiwais or any other tribe killing their neighbors with VK-98's or carbines or other guns."

"You yourself kill Kiwais with fast-shooting guns," Kokoda reminded Connors.

"Only to stop your slaughter of Bamus and others," I replied for Connors.

Kokoda now eyed me darkly. "You are a fine opponent, Rainey. I welcome the opportunity to fight against you. I did not come here to complain about our losses, or to plead with the white man. I am content to have you and Major Connors lead the Bamu. They need leadership. A victory over you and the major will not be a hollow one."

Kokoda gave Merah a sour look, but Merah

had apparently not understood enough of what Kokoda said to take offense.

"You intend to fight, then?" Connors asked heavily.

"Of course, Major. You have offered me a great challenge. When I win over you and Rainey, I will be a great chief. I will be spoken of in Kikori and even Port Moresby as the big chief of all upriver aborigines."

"Maybe there is some way to join Kiwais and Bamus without waging tribal war," I suggested.

Kokoda smiled tolerantly. "You know nothing of the aborigine, Rainey. We live to fight. It is like a religion to us. If Merah were stronger than me— if he had the guns—he would be busy killing Kiwais." He glanced toward the squatty Merah.

"Kiwais enemies of Bamus," Merah said simply.

"You see?" Kokoda said. "So if you were to defeat me, Merah would then kill Kiwais and subjugate them," Kokoda explained. "That is the way it is here, and no white man can change it."

"It does not have to be that way," I said slowly, "just because it always has been. Your world can change, just as the white man's does. There are many ways to prove courage and worth, other than with weapons. Some day men just like you, Kokoda, will help run the Port Moresby government—men who know the white man's language and ways, and who have courage."

Kokoda thought about that for a long moment, but Titimua interrupted the quiet. "White man from bik pella place talk-talk make Kokoda weak, make not want Bamu-war, he think-see Kiwai kill him and Bamu."

I suppose Titimua had reason to suspect our motives, knowing how strong Kokoda now was. Kokoda's face changed slightly, and he took on the old arrogant look again. "We came to talk about war, Rainey, and we will. The Kiwai will meet Merah and his Bamu with your weapons on the Kandam Plain, east of here, day after tomorrow, at dawn, in a tribal battle. If you do not come, we will come to your villages and find you."

Merah understood that. "We come make-war at Kandam place," he said darkly. "We win, make-dead many Kiwais."

Connors had suspected that this was what the talks had been directed toward. "Is this really what you want, Kokoda?" he now asked.

Kokoda nodded. "We look forward to it with great pleasure." He glanced toward Connors. "We also look forward to the removal of all white men from our territory—one way or the other," he told Connors grimly.

That was about the end of the talk. And I knew, as we left that jungle stream later, each side wary of the other in the physical parting, that that was probably the last time I would have the opportunity to get through to Kokoda with words alone. It would take something more than that.

When we returned to our headquarters and Merah announced the planned battle against the Kiwais, there was much excitement and jubilation. The Bamu warriors who knew how to fire a gun were enamored of their new power to kill, and felt indestructible.

In the next twenty-four hours, we tried to get more warriors ready to fight with guns. It was not easy, putting deadly weapons into those inexperienced hands. But in a small war, they would be better than axes and spears. We worked hard, and by the night of the next day, we classified almost a hundred warriors as riflemen. The arming of Merah and Zigibi and a few elders brought the total up to over a hundred, and then there were the Sten guns of our soldiers, and the grenades and mortars. But against that firepower we would probably have four or five hundred VK-98's, and a lot of spears and axes and machetes.

The odds were still definitely against us.

In the wee hours of the next morning, we moved out. We had to march three hours to the Kandam Plain, which was a low, flat area surrounded by hills, on the borderline between traditional Kiwai and Bamu territories. It was a battleground of long standing, where Kiwai and Bamu had met for centuries to let blood in the aborigine custom. It was considered hallowed ground.

When our little army arrived there, a couple hundred strong, it was still dark. We emerged onto the tall-grass meadow cautiously, and as our eyes focused on the open ground before us, we could see a mass of moving warriors across there. I could clearly see Kokoda at their fore, in his best feathered regalia.

As the sky gradually filled with light, and a blood-red sun climbed up over a low summit in the east, the scene materialized for us. Across the meadow the Kiwais stretched in a long, massive line, from one side to the other. Gazing over the dew-wet grass and low shrubbery that was peach-hued now on this pristine morning, I tried to guess the numbers of the enemy, and figured they must have six hundred men, and through binoculars I could see that two-thirds of them were armed with the damnable VK-98's. These troops had been put out in the front, and the spearmen with their brightly-painted shields were in the rear. Looking at that scene that lay stretched before me, I found myself reflecting that it had been this way for millennia. Except for the rifles.

I had used different strategy from Kokoda's. My spear and axe wielders, with their long skin shields and their weirdly made-up faces and the bone slivers in their noses, were out in front, and my riflemen were in the rear ranks. Ours was going to be a defensive battle in the initial stages, and my riflemen had to have protection because of their importance. I had put two mortar teams of Connors' men in the trees behind us, out of sight. Merah had objected to this strongly as against tradition, but I reminded him that the Volkssturms were not exactly traditional, either, nor the Stens and carbines. I had wanted to flank the field with hidden riflemen, too, but Merah objected so strongly, with backing of Zigibi and his elders, that I had to relent. Our Kikiro soldiers were spread out among the Bamu riflemen, as squad leaders, and all of them and Connors and I wore a thick ring of grenades around our waists, and bandoliers of ammo across our chests.

I hoped the grenades and mortars would be a big surprise to Kokoda, and that they might help us somehow hold our own against all those rifles Ruyker had sold him.

The sun rose above the hills and paled from red to yellow to a blazing white. The warriors on both sides now were chanting weird, tuneless chants across the open area between them, as part of the pre-game warm-up. The war would not begin until Merah and Kokoda gave the signal that it should, I knew. But the emotion was running high, and it would not be long. As the chanting became louder and more insistent, Connors came up to me, his face flushed already from the new morning heat and the excitement.

"The bloody fools!" he ranted. "Some of them don't even have ammo in the carbines yet! You wouldn't believe the chaos."

"I know," I said. "There are at least a couple of them who aren't exactly sure where the bullet exits from the gun. I wonder how it feels to be shot in the back by your own troops?"

Connors shook his head, his face pink under the Aussie hat. "Well, it's about time, Rainey. Are our mortars set?"

"They're ready," I said. "Thank God your people are trained in their use. They could make a difference."

Connors turned and watched our Bamu warriors—the ones with the spears, up front—chant their battle song and shake their spears toward the enemy. Then he turned back to me. "Good luck to you, old chap. It's good to have you out here with me. We're doing the only thing we can do, whether it works or not. The chaps in Kikori and Port Moresby had better bloody well hope it does, or Kokoda will be there one of these fine days."

I nodded. "Good luck to you, too, Connors. If it looks at any point as if we're going to be overrun, we'll withdraw from the field, rather than lose all the carbines to Kokoda."

"Agreed," Connors said. "We can't afford to let him—"

The chanting suddenly stopped on both sides, as if a button had turned it all off. Connors and I turned to see Merah strut out in front of his people, with a full regalia of feather headdress and cape. Kokoda had done the same on his side. They were now shouting some formal challenges to each other.

"Okay," Connors said tightly. "This is it."

Merah turned and strode proudly through his spearmen, and Kokoda, on the far side, did the same. At a mutual signal from both of them, then, the melee began.

There was a sudden yelling and whooping from both sides, and a lot of spear-waving, as Bamus and Kiwais advanced out toward the middle of the meadow, hurling insults at each other. There was no hostility at first, but then a rifle went off and a Bamu went down, and then a few Bamus screamed and began hurling spears. A Kiwai was hit in center chest, the spear piercing completely through him. He staggered in a tight circle, and fell, and then the Volkssturms began going off in earnest.

"Riflemen!" I yelled. *"Up and forward!"*

My squad leaders shouted commands, and the Bamu riflemen came running forward in long lines, toward the fighting at mid-field. But they stopped partway there, according to plan. The front rank knelt and waited, and the next rank came up behind them, in a standing position. They did not fire toward the melee.

"Hold your fire until they come to you!" I yelled down their ranks.

"Keep your positions firm!" Connors cried out.

Slattery was in charge of the entire line of standing riflemen, and Boggs was over the kneeling squads. Mixed in with the carbines were the Sten Mark V submachine guns of our Kikori troopers, and I hoped they, too, would be an experience worth remembering for Kokoda.

Now the riflemen of Kokoda were killing our spearmen fast. The two groups had charged and merged, and a few Kiwais were going down, and a lot of Bamus. Spearmen were shot in the chest and head, right through their colorful shields, while they tried to get their primitive weapons into play. They writhed on the ground, some of them, gut- and groin-shot. And now the Kiwais were getting through them and coming on toward our riflemen. I saw Kokoda give another loud command, from the rear, and more Kiwai riflemen swarmed out.

"Fall back!" I yelled toward the spearmen and axe-wielders now. *"Fall back fast!"*

Our people responded, when my orders were repeated to them, in Bamu. They turned and came back through the ranks of riflemen while the riflemen just stood and knelt and waited. Now the Kiwais were close enough to hit our riflemen, and a couple were hit. One man's face exploded as he knelt there, and another was hit in the high chest and twisted hard to his right, his weapon cracking into the leg of the man next to him and knocking him down. I swore under my breath, held my hand above my head as I looked toward the trees behind us, and then dropped my arm quickly to my side.

In the next instant the mortars boomed out in the morning air, with smoke rising from the trees. A few of the Kiwais stopped in their charge, then more of them. The first shell exploded violently in their rear ranks with a yellow flash and roar, and a dozen Kiwais flew in all directions. Another shell exploded, and several more Kiwais were hit.

The Kiwais were shocked by this. I looked and saw Kokoda, and his face was grim. Two more shells exploded, knocking down more Kiwais. Limbs had been torn from bodies, and holes torn out of chests. Great clouds of acrid smoke covered the field now, and some of the Kiwais were turning and running, to get out of the big explosions.

"Now!" I yelled. *"Commence firing!"*

While the confusion still reigned in the ranks of the Kiwais, our people now began firing the carbines and Stens. Automatic and semi-automatic fire raked the battlefield from two files of riflemen, and it was devastating. Kiwais were now going down fast, just as our spearmen had earlier. A few charged, anyway, and were mowed down by hot lead. Several came running wildly in my direction at the end of the defensive line, and I jerked a grenade loose and hurled it toward them. There was a violent explosion, and three of them flew through the air away from the center of it. Another fired several shots toward me, in dark anger, and one tore at my tunic. I leveled the Sten gun I carried in his direction, and blasted off a short blast, hitting him in the belly and chest, punching him off his feet.

Now others were hurling the grenades, too, and the violent explosions were having their effect. Kiwais were going down all across the field, and some of them were terrorized by these new and terrible weapons. The Stens rattled out their grim message over and over again, and the Kiwais were falling back. Some of our riflemen broke ranks against orders and ran toward the Kiwai lines, and were shot down. Kokoda was now shouting at his back-up warriors, some of whom had rifles, but most of whom were armed only with spears and axes. But there were a lot of them, and now they began responding to Kokoda's emotional yelling, and they came screaming wildly at us, outnumbering us three to one.

Some more grenades were loosed, killing several Kiwais at a time. But then they were on us, and the two small armies were engaged hand-to-hand, firing pointblank at each other. We could no longer use the mortars or even the grenades, but our carbines were deadly in comparison to the Volkssturms, and the Stens were murderous at close range. They came in wave after wave, reaching us in big groups and then merging with us, and the Stens rattled out their insistent message of death, cutting the enemy down one after the other.

It was hard to estimate which were the worst soldiers—ours or theirs. The Kiwais were lousy shots, just like the Bamus, and only hit targets half the time. Our people were able to fire faster, but I was not sure that was a blessing, because they were hitting each other with the carbines frequently. It was sheer chaos. But, amazingly, our people held their ground through that overwhelming attack for a long several minutes, before they began reluctantly to give ground. Slowly we were forced back as the hail of lead rained throughout the melee. I have no idea how I kept from getting hit through that, but I did. VK's and carbines alike were aimed right at me and fired, without hitting me. Merah, still wearing a sling on his right arm, had the same good luck. But Connors was not so fortunate. As we began falling back toward the south end of the battlefield, toward the hidden mortars, I saw Connors hit in the side by a VK-98 slug. He yelled slightly and thumped the ground hard, on his back, and there was a lot of blood on his green tunic. While he was still down there, without his Sten now, a Kiwai warrior raced up and aimed a rifle at his chest and fired. The fellow was a lousy shot, though, and the slug ripped into the flesh of Connors' arm instead of his chest. The fellow cocked the VK to fire again, and I raised my Sten gun and blasted off a few rounds at him. He was hit in the side, neck and head, and the back of his skull was blown off. He did a tight pirouette and fell onto a dead Bamu warrior.

"*Hold your ground!*" I yelled now at our people. We were still falling back under that savage onslaught by the strengthened Kiwais. "*Use those damned guns!*"

I stared hard through the smoke and melee, and saw several of our remaining Kikor troopers down. One had a long spear skewered through his neck, and another had been chopped to pieces, literally, by a steel axe. Slattery lay on top of a Kiwai warrior, with several bloody holes in his chest and back. Both of them were dead. The noncom Boggs was still firing his Sten, even though he was bleeding from the left arm and foot.

It was looking bad for us, despite our firepower. The numbers of the enemy were overpowering. I heard Boggs yelling at people around him now, to hold ground, and our remaining troopers were exhorting the Bamus in their own language to fight back. We had fallen back more than halfway to the trees behind us, but now, slowly, we began to hold our ground, taking more and more Kiwais down with our guns.

I raced to Connors, and he was grimacing in pain. *"Can you move?"* I yelled above the clamor.

He nodded, and struggled awkwardly to a sitting position. I grabbed his good arm and pulled him to his feet, and he leaned on me heavily. A Kiwai came and aimed a rifle at me, and I beat him with the Sten, almost blowing him in half with it. He jerked and danced backwards under the hail of hot lead, the VK-98 banging out into a brazen sky.

By the time I got Connors' arm around my shoulder, to help him to the rear, the war had reached a bloody stalemate, with heavy killing and neither side gaining ground. A couple more of our Kikori soldiers went down, and I could see only one left. They had more than earned their battle pay. I staggered toward the trees with Connors, to try to keep him from getting his head blown off. By the time I got to the rear ranks of Bamus, though, the shooting had quieted some, and I saw that Kokoda had ordered a withdrawal to his side of the field.

"Cease fire!" I yelled loudly, with Connors still hanging on me. *"Pull back!"*

In the next few minutes, the firing stopped completely, and both sides withdrew out of effective range. Out there in the middle of the battleground were strewn the dead and dying, and it was a grisly sight. The Sten guns and carbines had really hacked the Kiwais up badly, and their steel axes had done a bloody job on our people. There were parts of bodies lying about everywhere, and terrible mutilations. Wounded men sat and screamed in pools of their own blood, and many corpses had been beheaded, with both sides keeping a trophy pile. The new silence across the field was punctuated by the screams and moans of the wounded and dying.

But, for the moment, it was over.

Connors had been put on a crude stretcher, and was in bad shape. He had lost a lot of blood. But he looked over to me now, and grinned with his sweaty face. "We did it, Rainey. We held them, by God!"

I nodded, then stared out across the field, to where I could see Kokoda staring back grimly toward me. He was obviously calling it a day. But I wondered what was going through that half-civilized savage head. It would undoubtedly occur to him, now, to do what we had done—gather many more Kiwais around him than he now had, drawing on all his resources. If he did, he could crush us with just weight of numbers.

It was just possible that only the first act of this primitive drama had been played out.

With the end very much in question.

NINE

We straggled back to home base all through the rest of that day. Even though we had held Kokoda to a stalemate out on that battleground, we had suffered terrible losses. We returned with less than fifty percent of our forces intact.

It was a long, ugly march back, one I will never forget. Connors passed out a couple of times and I was worried that I would lose him. Boggs was injured, too, and hobbled back looking very dejected. Only our private soldier, a small, wiry-looking fellow, was unhurt but looked afraid to fight again. He had been through a real hell. Merah was in high spirits, because we had stood up to Kokoda and the Kiwai. The heads his men had gathered were carried back to headquarters on short poles, in way of celebration, and Merah kept saying that we had won the war with the Kiwai. I knew that was not true.

Kokoda had waited until we left the field to retire his own warriors from it, probably to save some face. He had made no further communication with us, either personally or formally. He was making us guess what was in his dark head, and I did not like that very much.

When we arrived back at the Bamu village, we

were greeted by those who had stayed behind as conquering heroes. Zigibi wore the grotesque wooden mask and did a dance around Merah and me, praising and thanking Bamu gods for their help. The Kiwai heads were hoisted to the tops of tall trophy poles, and there was a lot of excitement in general. No one mourned the dead. There was no suggestion, even, that Merah would send anybody back to bury them. That was the way it was in the jungle.

I put Connors on a makeshift cot in our large open hut, and his wounds were re-bandaged by me and our remaining private. Boggs was fitted with a cane. As soon as Connors was through with the bandaging, he fell unconscious and slept heavily.

For the next twenty-four hours, I was not sure that Connors would make it. The lead in his side had busted a floating rib and torn up a lot of flesh, although it apparently had not hit a vital organ before exiting several inches further back. That was what was causing him the most trouble. The arm wound in his left biceps was shallow, but undoubtedly painful as hell.

Our position was not a good one, now. Even with the warriors we had left behind to guard the village, our numbers were drastically reduced, for a second fight, should Kokoda press one on us. And just as important, we had lost Connors for all practical purposes, Slattery, and all but one of our tough-as-nails troopers from Kikori. Leadership, therefore, had been almost eliminated in our first, indecisive battle of our war. Lastly, we had lost several carbines and Sten guns to Kokoda in the melee, reducing our arms and adding to his.

Merah ignored all this, though, and insisted on

acting the part of a triumphant general. There was a big celebration in the village that evening, with dancing, chanting and drums. Some warrior had brought back a Kiwai corpse without my knowledge, and parts of it were cooked on an open fire. Connors was in no condition to object, and I did not give a damn. Halfway through the evening, I passed the big hut we had erected for our own use, and saw that Connors was awake. I decided we needed a palaver.

"How are you feeling?" I asked him as I sat down beside his cot, on a stump stool. Connors' private was nearby, watching over him. He was slumped against a hut pole, on the ground, and took little notice of us.

"Not so bad, Rainey," he grinned weakly. "Considering."

"You need medical help," I said seriously. "And a hospital bed. I think we have to return to Kikori."

Connors' face darkened. "Return? Have you gone round the bend on me, Rainey? Good God, man, we've got Kokoda on the run! Did you see his face out there today, after the fighting? We gave him something to think about, by Jesus!"

Connors was weak from that little tirade. I shook my head slowly. "Major, Kokoda is not beaten, by a long way. He lost more people than we did out there this morning, but he could afford to. He probably still has us three to one, and he can raise it considerably from that, by just doing some recruiting like we've done. He was impressed by the mortars and grenades and Stens, but he was not terrorized by them. He knows he's seen our worst now, and he lasted through it."

"But my God, Rainey, I can't leave now! I have to see this all out."

"You're in no shape to fight," I told him. "You could die, you know. And I can't send you back to the river with just your private here. I'd have to go."

"That's just it, old man. These people can't afford to lose you now. Merah doesn't know it, of course, but this is a critical juncture. We can't just abandon them now to Kokoda's wrath. Even if we left the carbines—which I would never consider seriously—they would have no chance against Kokoda without leadership. We would be leaving them worse off than they were before."

I knew that Connors was right. But so was I. He was in serious condition. In the shape he had gotten in, jungle bacteria could kill him very quickly. And it would take weeks for recovery from his wounds, if he made it.

I rose from the seat, and strode up and down beside the cot. "I don't know, Connors. At this moment, saving these savages from each other doesn't seem worth even one more life like yours." I stopped, and turned to him. "But you should be entitled to the controlling vote, where your own life is concerned. If you want to stay, we stay."

Connors grinned weakly. "Thanks, Rainey. I do appreciate your understanding."

I looked down at the bloody bandage on his side, and grunted. "I hope it all comes out all right, Connors."

"Maybe it will," he said. "Why don't we send a runner to Kokoda, and do a little chest-beating? We may never have a better chance to scare him off. Tell him that we have a lot more weapons

than he saw today—a little lie never hurt, in war—
and that we want to prevent more Kiwai deaths.
Tell him we seek another talk. About disarmament."

I shrugged. "It can't hurt. I'll see to it."

The next morning, we sent a runner out to neutral territory. Merah and Zigibi were against offering Kokoda a peace talk, but Connors and I prevailed. I wondered just how difficult it might be, now, to take the carbines back from Merah, with our regular army squad half knocked out and Connors injured.

After the runner was sent out, the rest of the day was spent in planning recruitment of a last few hold-out Bamus who were still sticking it out in separate small villages. Boggs, although injured himself, helped the half-caste private soldier and a few well-chosen Bamu warriors continue training the rest of them. Connors rested quietly all day, with a Bamu woman assigned to keep the flies and other insects off him. In late afternoon, when I was still out beside the village on the rifle range, Boggs came to me and reported that Connors wanted to see me.

"The runner is back, Major," he explained.

I wiped sweat from my brow and strode back into the village. The sun was hot, and the trophy heads had begun to stink, and the big blood-sucking flies were everywhere. I would be glad when it was all over, one way or another. I found Connors sitting up on his cot, propped on a crate and bedding. His face was grim. Outside the hut, Merah and Zigibi were talking together animatedly, with Zigibi wearing an angry scowl.

"What is it?" I asked Connors.

He sighed. "Sit down, Rainey."

I seated myself beside the cot, and Connors adjusted himself painfully to a more comfortable position. "We've got our answer from Kokoda," he said. "You might call it a negative one."

"What did he say?"

"You were right, Rainey," Connors said. "He's been out recruiting, and he boasts a new, bigger army."

"Christ!"

"He says he's gathered a thousand warriors around him. So you can figure maybe seven or eight hundred," Connors went on. "He also says he captured twenty of our guns. We only lost a dozen, didn't we?"

I nodded. "Maybe a couple more than that."

"He was miffed by the mortars and grenades," Connors went on. "The bloody fool says we fought unfair."

I shook my head. "That's the best I've heard in some time." I waved a hand at a big fly that was buzzing around my face.

"He says our mortars defiled his battlefield. Says he's coming here next time, to wipe out the village once and for all. Wants to destroy the Bamus as a race. And he wants our heads."

"Hmmph," I said.

"If he makes good on his threat, Rainey," Connors told me, "he'll put every man, woman and child in danger of a bloody death. There's no damned place else to send them, where they would be safe."

"I know," I said. "Did he say when he was coming?"

Connors made a wry face. "Soon."

I took in a deep breath, and let it out slowly. The fat was in the fire now. Kokoda intended to make it a fight for tribal survival, and it was difficult to think of any persuasion that would dissuade him.

"Maybe you'd better try to make it to the river without me," I said heavily. "Take your private and a Bamu warrior as litter-carriers. They'll get you there without incident, probably. If you stay here, you'll be a sitting duck when the Kiwais come."

"A bloody liability, is what you mean," Connors grinned.

"That, too." I wanted him safe downriver.

He shook his head, his ruddy face firm with conviction and determination. "That won't do it, Rainey. I know you need me here, whether you do or not. I can understand what old Merah is saying, for one thing. No, I'm staying, all right."

"Are you damned sure?" I asked him somberly.

He nodded. "Damned sure." He glanced out toward where Merah and Zigibi discussed hotly in the sun. "Merah has to be kept in line. I can help. He wants to attack Kokoda, for God's sake. Can you imagine the result of that?"

I looked from Merah to Connors. "Okay, Major. It's your trophy head."

Connors grinned again. "Oh, I almost forgot to tell you. Kokoda says he's captured Ruyker."

"Oh, oh,". I muttered.

"He says that Ruyker is going to suffer the same fate as every other white man who meddles in tribal affairs."

"I think he's trying to tell us something."

"Yes, it would seem. That bloody fool Ruyker may be finished with gun-selling, anyway."

"I would guess that about now, he's wishing he was in your jail at Kikori," I suggested.

We stepped up our training program, that very afternoon, and I put about fifty Bamus at work building low defensive barriers around the perimeter of the village, embankments of logs and earth that we raised to chest height, like a low wall. It would be behind those barriers that we would make our stand. Behind the first line of defense we also raised a broken line of secondary barriers, to fall back to. We worked all that night and through the next morning, hoping to beat Kokoda's timetable, whatever it was.

All through that next day, stragglers came in from the remaining villages of Bamus in the vicinity. Most were women and children, but we added a few men to our ranks. I figured we would have close to a hundred riflemen when Kokoda came, and another fifty warriors with primitive weapons. Kokoda would probably have four or five times that number, if his recruitment was as successful as Connors expected.

The women and children were gathered in the two large huts at the center of the village, and bamboo sides were erected on these structures, to keep stray bullets out. It would give some protection to them. Merah, under my orders, instructed them to rush to these huts at the first sign of the enemy—those who might be out in the open—and stay there until it was over.

Kokoda did not come that day, nor the next. The unnerving thing about it was that he could come at any moment, or wait for weeks. We had to play his game, because we just did not have the strength to go on the offensive. Also, I knew that a good defender can make a siege an expensive proposition for the besieging force. Good armies have been destroyed trying to take a well-defended fortress, and I hoped we could emulate those earlier defenders who had proved that point.

On the third day after Kokoda's message to us, a second one came, in late afternoon. One of our patrols came back with a Kiwai girl in tow. Connors and I were in the smaller enclosed hut, conferring about strategy. We had shooed the women and children out, for privacy. Merah brought the girl in to us, with Zigibi attending.

"What's all this?" Connors asked Merah. Connors was now sitting up for a while through the day, trying to heal his wounds. He seemed indestructible.

Zigibi held the Kiwai girl tightly by her arm, and her hands were bound behind her. He seemed to have assumed a proprietary interest over her.

"Kokoda send last talk-talk, also gifts for the Major Rainey," Merah explained to us.

"Gifts?" I asked.

"It's a custom between warring tribes," Connors said. "I believe the girl is yours."

Merah now lapsed into Bamu, talking very fast, his broad face serious, and the ugly Zigibi put in a few words, too. I did not understand what they were saying. Finally Connors turned to me.

"The message from Kokoda is that he will arrive here with a massive army early tomorrow. He intends to wipe out every man, woman and child he finds here. He will deem it a great honor to capture your head and mine. Particularly yours."

"I'm beginning to feel a little like a prize hog at a county fair," I said sourly.

"Kokoda has you figured as a great general," Connors grinned. "It's quite a compliment to you."

"I'd just as soon he kept his compliments," I commented, "and I kept my head." I glanced toward the girl. She was young, not many years past puberty, and wore only a lap-lap around her hips. Her breasts and thighs were chocolate-delicious-looking, and her face was rather attractive for an aborigine. "What does she have to do with all this?"

"She is a personal gift from Kokoda to you," Connors said, his face going serious now. "That's what all the rhubarb is about. Zigibi thinks this is a slight to Merah. He wants you to give the girl over to the village."

"What the hell for?"

Now Connors' face was even more grim. "I know this will be hard for you to understand, Rainey. But she was sent for a feast."

I knitted my brow. "She's going to be the guest-of-honor stand-in for Kokoda?"

Connors shook his head. "She's to be the bloody meal."

My jaw dropped slightly.

"She's your to butcher, like a lamb," Connors said gravely. "And Merah and Zigibi are looking forward to it already. Thigh of tender maiden is a delicacy in these parts."

"Sonofabitch," I mumbled.

I studied the girl's face for the first time. There was a kind of numbness in it, as if she had put herself into a trance, to get through what was coming for her. I swallowed hard.

"Tell Merah that if he wants a thigh to chew on, he can start on Zigibi's," I growled.

Merah was watching my grim face, but did not understand. Zigibi stood scowling behind him, with the girl.

"I think I'd better improve on that in the translation," Connors said. He turned to Merah and spoke in Bamu, and there was a long silence when he was finished, and then some loud talk from Zigibi. Connors shouted back at Zigibi, and Merah spoke to Connors in a more rational manner, and finally Zigibi released the girl and stalked out of the hut. Merah said a few more words to Connors, eyed me a bit hostilely, and followed Zigibi out.

Connors turned to me, grimacing with pain in his side. "Well, the girl is spared. I told them you wished to have her for a slave, rather than a meal. Zigibi thought that that would cheat the Bamus out of a fine celebration, and was quite put out. Merah admitted that you have the right to do what you want with the girl, but said he had expected better of you."

I shook my head slowly. "I sure as hell didn't need this now. What do we do with her?"

Connors shrugged. "She belongs to you, Rainey. Think of something," he said, half-grinning. He rose unsteadily. "I'll go talk further with Merah. I need to use the old legs a bit. Umm. I'll knock on my return, old chap."

I started to protest, but then Connors was gone. We had hung a piece of burlap over the hut entrance, so that the girl and I now had some privacy. I had just gotten up to try to tell her to sit down somewhere, when Connors poked his head back in, and said something in Kiwai to the girl, then grinned at me. "I just told her she'll live, and that you're her benefactor," he said, then disappeared again.

"Connors!" I called after him.

But he was gone. I turned to the girl, and a new look had come into her face. She looked human again, rather than like a robot. The relief that came over her was overwhelming. If she had been a civilized girl, I am certain that she would have cried and broken down completely. But she had been raised not to show that kind of emotion. She came over to me now, the breasts moving as she walked. She was sensual in her way. I suppose that if I had been isolated in the bush for six months, she might even have looked beautiful. She began talking in Kiwai, and I could not understand a word.

"I'm sorry," I said. "I don't understand." I put a hand on her shoulder, and suddenly that created an intimacy between us in her mind.

She came and pressed her nakedness against me in a way that is known to girls everywhere, aborigine or Fifth Avenue model. She was not Nellie Waki, but I cannot say it was unpleasant. She spoke some more to me, more softly, and I got the idea without knowing the language. I was being propositioned. She was my slave, so she was suggesting a nice way to start out our master-servant relationship.

"No," I said. "I have a war to fight."

She did not understand a word. I felt tired suddenly. I went and sat on a cot, and she came and knelt beside me, smiling pleasantly. She said some words in Kiwai, and gestured for me to lie down. I felt like it. I put my head down on the bedroll-pillow, and she lifted my feet up. Suddenly I was king. To one girl, anyway. I thought I would have a short rest while I ran over alternate defense strategies in my head. But then the Kiwai maiden was unfastening my trousers.

She had an instinctive feeling for getting civilized clothing unfastened in a hurry. I did not stop her. She did nice things to me then, without ever getting onto the cot with me. There was a smell about her that some men might have found offensive, but that at that moment seemed earthy and sensual to me. All she ever got around to were things I had always considered preliminaries, but that kind of love-making did the job there on that cot in the dimness of the communal hut. Before I knew how far it had gone, there was a sudden trembling inside me, an expectation of fulfillment, and then a surging, muscle-tensing moment when all the pent-up tension flowed out of me and was replaced by a dark and quiescent calm.

When Connors returned, in a half-hour, I had somehow gotten across to the Kiwai girl that her safety depended on her remaining in that hut with the women and children, and attracting as little attention as possible until the coming battle was finished. So when Connors entered the hut, she was sitting in a corner, keeping out of the way. She was satisfied because she had already rewarded me for keeping her off a fire spit.

Connors was grim-faced when he came in. He looked at the girl briefly, then spoke to me. "I see you've got her behaving," he said.

I nodded. "You look like you've seen Kokoda's

ghost. What's the matter?"

Connors sighed. "You may recall that Merah indicated there was more than one gift from Kokoda to you."

I thought back. Merah had, in fact, used the plural "gifts" when he announced the presence of the girl. "Yes, I guess so," I said.

"Well, there is another one," Connors said. "Merah has had it brought up outside the hut. Maybe you ought to take a look."

I gave Connors a quizzical look, and then shrugged. Walking past him to the covered entranceway, I stooped and pushed the burlap back and went outside, with Connors right behind me.

When I got out in the sunlight, I saw what Kokoda had sent as his second gift. Merah and Zigibi stood there, with several elders, and two warriors held a new trophy pole erect. All present looked at me for a moment, then turned their eyes on the top of the trophy pole. I did the same.

My jaw dropped even further than it had when I learned what Kokoda expected me to do with the Kiwai maiden.

"Good Jesus!" I muttered numbly.

On the top of the trophy pole was a freshly-decapitated bloody head, but this display was special. Down below the head were two short crossbars, with severed arms and legs hanging wired to them, so that the whole display resembled a grotesque stick-figure of wood and mangled flesh. On the head itself, a part of the right ear was missing from an old injury, and there was a scar across the left eye that gave a hard look to the square face, even in death. The eyes were wide open, staring out into the thick jungle that the man had traversed repeatedly for ten years, making his dark deals with the natives.

The butchered remains on the pole were those of Hendrik Ruyker.

TEN

Of course, Ruyker had not been the kind of fellow that either Connors or I would have chosen as Man of the Year in New Guinea. He had been a soulless bastard whose greed had been responsible for sheer, bloody chaos in that primitive world, a man whose own mother could not have liked him. He had given Connors fits over the years, and had tried to kill me on two separate occasions. But seeing his mutilated parts on that pole sent a shiver down my spine that lasted all through that night of waiting for Kokoda to come. Ruyker had been, after all, a white man in that aborigine jungle, and so were Connors and I. His ignominious end, I knew, just might befall both of us yet.

I was much more shocked by that display than I had been by seeing Ardrey's severed head. In addition to the extra bloodiness of this, there was the fact that I had thought, deep inside, that Ruyker would somehow double-talk his way around Kokoda. But now it was painfully clear that Kokoda was not a man to be side-tracked from an idea, once it got firmly into his head. And his head told him that it wanted mine.

Again I incurred Zigibi's wrath by demanding that Ruyker's remains be taken from the pole, and buried. Connors thought I was wrong in insisting, after saving the girl, but I had had it with stone-age ritual. If these people wanted my help against Kokoda, they could do something to please me just occasionally. Connors said, that night, that Zigibi was busy making threats to Merah about me, and I told him I did not give a damn.

That night was a short one. I lay down on a bedroll near Connors' and Boggs' cots, outside the bit huts, at about one a.m. The women and children now occupied the big huts, and were not often allowed outside them. We put a light guard on duty at the perimeter, out well past the barriers, to make sure we were not surprised in the night. But everything went very quietly. I slept until about four-thirty, and then got up to get things organized.

Connors had sacked out much earlier because he needed the rest. He was up, though, at five, and was walking around much better. He insisted on being issued a Sten, and taking his place in the ranks of the defenders. Boggs was recuperating well, limping about on a bad foot and wearing a bandage on his arm. The one private soldier we had left was everywhere, shouting orders in Bamu, doing a great job. Merah and Zigibi mostly just watched sullenly, probably thinking they no longer needed Connors and me, with the guns. Merah could not have been more wrong. Left to his own devices, he would have made no defense at all against a well-organized assault. I wondered if we would be able to survive it, even with Connors and me directing the defense.

At dawn we were entrenched behind our barricades. Empty ammo boxes and gun crates had been added to the log and dirt embankments, filling in gaps in our defensive wall. Every available man was now stationed behind it, in readiness. We concentrated our people on the north of the village, because that was where we figured Kokoda would come from, and we were right. At just after dawn, a scout came running in from the jungle, his eyes wild. He had just spotted Kokoda's warrior army, and they would be there within ten minutes.

"Well," Connors grinned, leaning on a barricade beside me, looking almost well now, but slightly pale. "This is the showdown, old sport. This ought to go until one side or the other is done for."

"That's what I'm afraid of," I admitted.

The women were all inside the big huts and out of sight. The Bamu warriors lined the barricades, looking tough but a little unsure. They had reason to be.

The first Kiwais that showed up emerged from a forest clearing adjacent to the village and about fifty yards across. At first it did not appear that there were so many of them, but then they kept coming out into view, in twos and threes. Soon there was a long line of them across the clearing, with the trees in back of them, and we could see more stacked up in back of them in the trees. From the sound and movement over there, it appeared that Connors' guess would be right. There appeared to be at least seven hundred of them. We were outnumbered five to one.

"Good God, would you look at them!" Connors whistled. "I don't think I've ever seen so many fuzzy heads all in one place."

"Kokoda probably got a hell of a lot more

Volkssturm rifles from Ruyker before he killed him, too," I said. "Every Kiwai in sight has a gun."

"I see a couple of our Stens out there," Connors commented glumly.

Merah came up beside us, wearing his battle regalia again. He had appropriated a Sten gun for himself, since the loss of our Kikori troops, and now carried it awkwardly at his side. We had not objected, because he had suffered enough loss of face. But I did not much like him getting behind me with that thing.

"Kiwai come," he observed somberly. "Kokoda make too-big army. We stay-wait much-long days, he strong now."

I presumed that that was a critical remark, but ignored it. There had not been anything to do to prevent Kokoda from organizing his people the way we had organized Merah's. We had saved our strength for this all-out assault by Kokoda, and I could only hope that somehow we might survive it.

I held a pair of binoculars to my eyes. The sun was rising from behind a low hill to the east now, and visibility was good. Kokoda was out in sight, moving toward his front ranks. He, too, was dressed gaudily in feathers and shells, and his face was brightly painted in red and white. He lifted his arm now for quiet among his warriors, and a silence fell over the massed assemblage around him. Then he was shouting across the clearing to us, in Kiwai. He shouted and waved his Enfield rifle for several minutes, and then there was an answering clamor from his warriors that reverberated across the clearing.

"What was all that about?" I asked Connors.

Connors grunted. "He said the battle will be over when all Bamus are dead, and the white men's heads decorate his trophy poles."

I made a face. "Well, you have to hand it to him. It took some character to come back like this after what he saw our mortars and grenades do to his people the last time."

"He knows well the advantage of numbers," Connors said. "If he had known we're out of mortar shells and that our grenades are now at a minimum, he might have come even sooner."

"Thank God we brought more ammo for the carbines than we thought we'd ever use," I said. "We don't have that much left for the Stens."

Merah was out beyond the fortifications now, responding to Kokoda's threat, and I hoped that some over-eager Kiwai did not blow his ugly head off. That would create complete anarchy in our ranks, in all probability.

"You stay put, Major," I told Connors. "You can't get around well enough to move about much. All right?"

"I'll try to keep out of your way, Rainey," he grinned.

I left Connors back near the big huts, and walked to the barriers. There was a lot of shouting and yelling from both sides now, but the Bamus understood well that they were badly outnumbered. That did not stop them from working themselves up into a frenzy, though, and a few of them broke ranks and ran out into the small clearing. Kiwai rifles cut them down, and we lost them.

"Merah!" I yelled to him nearby. *"Keep them under control! It's our only chance!"*

The yelling quieted down some then, and a

deadly kind of chanting came from the Kiwai ranks, as they prepared themselves mentally for the attack.

I had no idea how long all of that would continue, but I figured Kokoda wanted to wear our nerves down some, so it might go on quite some time. I paced the compound, waiting, trying not to hear that primitive chanting. Connors hobbled over to me from the far side of the village in the middle of all that, and his face was grim.

"Everything all right on the far perimeter?" I asked.

"Our ranks are holding steady," he said. "But I'm having trouble with Zigibi. The bloke seems to be going round the bend on us, I'm afraid. He asked again if he could have the Kiwai girl, and I told him no, and he seemed quite upset. Now they've captured a Kiwai warrior."

I was surprised. "How the hell did they manage that?"

"The poor fellow had come sneaking up to have a look at our strength, I suppose. Zigibi is interrogating him, if you can call it that. I believe Merah is on his way there to supervise. It's pretty bloody, Rainey. I tried to stop it, but Zigibi shouted me down."

"What are they doing to him?" I said.

"You'd better have a look for yourself," Connors told me.

I stared across the village compound where some warriors were gathered behind a hut. A scream came from that direction, above the clamor of shouting and chanting from our side.

"I'll take a look," I said. "We don't have the time or manpower for Zigibi's diversions."

I strode across the compound, with Connors coming up behind me. When I got to the hut where the warriors were gathered, I elbowed my way in past them, and they scattered quickly for me. In the center of the gathering was the Kiwai warrior, tied to a post as I had been at the Kiwai village. Merah and Zigibi stood close to him, and a Bamu warrior was cutting on him with a very sharp machete. They had opened him up like a can of peas, and there was blood everywhere. Internal organs hung outside his torso, and his eyes were glazing over, but he was in agony.

"What is this, Merah?" I said loudly.

Merah turned to me, and so did Zigibi. Zigibi's face was full of emotion. Merah spoke to me arrogantly in Bamu, and Connors, who now came up beside me, translated.

"He says Zigibi is questioning the prisoner, to find out what Kokoda's strategy is," Connors said.

"Good God," I muttered. "What do they think they'll find out? Look at that poor sonofabitch."

"I know," Connors said.

"Get away from that man," I told them, darkly. The sight of what they had done to him was making me slightly nauseous.

Zigibi shouted something at me, and nobody moved. I raised the Sten gun I was carrying, and Merah took a couple of steps away from it. Zigibi was already out of my line of fire. The warrior who had cut up the Kiwai stayed where he was, under Zigibi's orders. I squeezed the trigger of the Sten, and it banged out a short, violent tattoo above the clamor around us.

The slugs punched the Bamu warrior in the

chest and abdomen, knocking him off his feet, and then tore into the dying Kiwai, punching into the exposed guts and organs, killing him instantly and putting him out of his misery.

Even Connors was surprised by my action. Zigibi's and Merah's mouths fell open, and there was a sudden silence in our part of the compound. The Sten smoked in my hand.

I turned to Merah. "I am the general in charge now," I said simply. "I'll say how prisoners will be interrogated, and when. My life is on the line here, as is Major Connors'. We have no time for this kind of thing. We must now fight for our lives."

Quite suddenly, Zigibi reacted. He came and began shouting Bamu obscenities into my face, and gesturing wildly, his ugly face full of hatred.

"What is he saying?" I asked Connors.

"Best not to repeat most of it, old boy," Connors said tightly. "He's overwrought, all right. He says you're not fit for command, and challenges you to the right to lead the Bamus in battle."

"To hell with that," I growled. "This idiot wants to play games while the Kiwais plot our deaths. I ought to shoot the bastard and end it."

Merah said a few comforting words to Zigibi, then gave me a hard look. "Zigibi make challenge to you for make-war, you take-up, okay?"

Connors regarded me balefully. "I'm afraid you're going to have to face up to this, Rainey. Merah is behind him."

I glared at Merah, and then at his ugly broadnosed priest. "How much time do we have before Kokoda gets his people worked up enough to come in?" I asked Connors.

"It won't be immediately." He furrowed his brow. "Rainey, I didn't mean for you to accept Zigibi's challenge. We can palaver, make concessions, let Zigibi save face."

"There isn't time for all of that," I said. "And I can't be harassed by this bastard through this. Tell them I'll accept his challenge."

"That will mean a physical contest," Connors warned me, "with primitive weapons."

I nodded understanding. "Let's do it."

Connors spoke to them in Bamu, and when they understood, Merah grinned slightly. Zigibi shouted something else into my face, and then Merah was ordering his warriors to get weapons for us, and a small ring of Bamus formed around us very quickly.

"See that the big share of our people stays out at the barricades," I told Connors as I turned my Sten over to him.

He nodded. "Are you sure you want this, Rainey? Zigibi may be smaller than you, but he's tough as nails, and he knows primitive weapons."

"I'm sure," I said.

Connors gave orders to subordinates to keep the troops of Merah on the front lines of defense, and two ugly warriors brought Zigibi and I our weapons. We were each given a small hand axe, and a machete. Merah came out into the small circle and wished us both good luck in Bamu, but I knew whom he was rooting for. I saw Connors' face in the circle of dark ones, and also that of Boggs. They looked as worried as I felt.

Zigibi and I were ready. With a small shout of anger, the Bamu priest jumped closer to me, wielding the axe and machete. I stepped back slightly as he swung the machete toward me in a wide arc, and I could hear its soft hissing through the air. One good connection with either of those cutting weapons could kill or disable me. I began circling Zigibi and his dark eyes narrowed on me.

There was some shouting now from the Bamus around us, and behind Zigibi I could see the mutilated body of the Kiwai warrior in the hot sun, grim evidence of Zigibi's skill with cutting edges. I saw a small opening, and swung the hand axe at Zigibi's face, and he hopped away with surprising agility. He had assumed a low crouch, and was almost impossible to get to in that position because he made a small target. Zigibi now did some very fancy stepping, gaining confidence, dancing in a circle around me and swinging the axe and machete alternately as he went. I turned and tried to keep facing him, knowing how quickly one of those blades could find an opening and slice me into little pieces. I swung the machete now, with its longer sweep, and almost got Zigibi's shoulder, and he jumped back, his face going more somber.

"What's the matter, Zigibi?" I growled toward him. "Don't you like it when your opponents fight back?"

He did not understand the words, but the meaning did not escape him. He swung the two weapons in an almost simultaneous motion, with the machete coming hard on the arc of the axe, and I had a hell of a time getting out of the way. He did some dancing, and moved around me so quickly it was difficult to follow him, and then attacked again. He feinted with the axe, and then swung the machete viciously toward my torso, intending to split me in two. I twisted hard away, and the blade ripped through my tunic at my side and grazed my flesh there, like a hot iron.

I gasped and stumbled backwards, and the axe came. I warded it off with my machete, the two blades clashing loudly in the clearing, and then I stumbled backwards and fell onto my back. In a split-second, Zigibi stood over me with an unnerving grin on his ugly face, the machete above his head. He brought it down in a savage stroke to decapitate me, and I rolled aside and the blade thumped the hard dirt beside my left ear. In the same instant, I swung the machete in my right hand at Zibigi's left knee. He did not see the counter-attack in time and I connected. The blade cut through fles and tendon and bone and severed his leg just below the knee.

Blood sprayed into my face as Zigibi's leg fell away from him, and he stood for a moment in shock, then toppled beside me. I thought it might be over then, but now Zigibi awkwardly swung the axe at my head. I blocked it with the machete I had just cut his leg off with, and the weapon was knocked from my grasp. I rose off the ground and swung the axe in my left hand in one motion, at Zigibi's head. He partially deflected it, but it still hit him in the side of the face. It thumped hard there, burying itself in his head.

Zigibi shuddered through the length of his body, and then lay motionless beside me.

The warriors around the circle were very quiet. I could hear Kokoda's Kiwais in the background, building to a high emotional pitch, and figured the attack was ready. If these people did not accept me as their military leader, we were in trouble. But then, one at a time, they shouted their praise to me for my victory over Zigibi.

Connors came over to me as I got to my feet. "You did it, Rainey. Are you all right?"

I nodded. The flesh wound on my side was just a scratch. "I'll be okay."

Merah came out into the circle, looked sourly down at the dead Zigibi with the axe still protruding from his head, and then turned to me. "You too-much big warrior, Rainey. You lead Bamu in end-war against Kiwai."

Without Zigibi around to inflame him against me, Merah was finally accepting me as his military leader. I made a face, listening to Kokoda's drums and chanting in the background of this primitive morning.

"Let's just hope that will give you some small advantage," I said heavily to Merah. "Because you're going to need it. All of us are."

ELEVEN

As I finished that pronouncement to Merah, there was a sudden and tumultuous uproar from the Kiwais all around us, and then it began. Kokoda was attacking.

We were galvanized into action.

"To the barricades!" I yelled. *"Get behind the barricades!"*

"Hold your fire until they're right on you!" Connors shouted toward Boggs and his last Kikori trooper, and then he repeated it in Bamu, as our people gathered behind the barricades and the few women left out in the open were herded into the big huts.

I raced to the barricades where the main attack was coming from, and saw that the Kiwais were coming in force. The hot morning air was rent with the banging of rifles and the occasional fire of Stens. We had a few mortar shells left, and a few grenades, and we now let them all go in a show of strength that we hoped would scare the Kiwais. But it did not. Back in their rear ranks, big groups of warriors were downed by the violent yellow explosions, but then suddenly we were out of grenades and shells, and we had hardly made a dent in their ranks.

The first wave of Kiwais had hit us hard, and most of them now lay dead before the barriers, hit with rifle and Sten fire. A few had gotten over the barriers and killed some Bamus before being killed themselves and terribly mutilated by our people after they were down. It was hard as hell to get the Bamus to kill and then forget the encounter and go on to another of the enemy. They always wanted to maul and savage the body, if it was within reach.

The second wave was hitting us now, and the battle was getting even more fierce than the one on the plain. Kiwais were beginning to hit their marks, and more of them were getting past the barricades and into the village. I looked down the row of dark, fuzzy heads, and saw that there were already fewer of us. Their numbers were overwhelming us. I turned and saw a whole swarm of Kiwais heading right at my position. I opened up with the Sten, and it raked across their ranks savagely, knocking them down one after the other. One got through and came firing wildly at me. A slug tore at my sleeve and then he was leaping the barrier, jumping on me with the butt end of the rifle swinging toward my head. I ducked and deflected the blow and we went down together, rolling in the dust behind the barricade. I finally slammed the barrel of the Sten against his face hard, crushing it in, and he fell off me, kicking and jerking on the ground.

Now they were really coming. More and more Kiwais were getting past the barriers, and a lot of Bamus were going down, shot through the face and head and chest. It was bloody as hell. The gunfire was so deafening that you could not hear your own voice above it. It was the climax of the only modern war this jungle had ever seen, and it was amazing how quickly these primitive men took to modern weaponry. It was also frightening.

"Keep firing!" I found myself yelling over and over. *"Kill the riflemen first! Silence their guns!"*

Kokoda was sending his spearmen in with the riflemen now, with their colorful shields and fierce war-paint, and because there were so many of them, they were getting behind the lines and giving us fits. Bamus were being run through with spears from the back while they were firing toward attacking riflemen. Others were being decapitated with machetes and axes before they could turn to defend their backs. I saw a couple of spearmen run toward the nearest big hut with flaming torches, and swore under my breath. They must have learned or guessed that the women and children were gathered in those primitive buildings.

I headed toward the hut, and almost stumbled over a body. Looking down at it through the haze of acrid gunsmoke, I saw that it was Boggs—the last white man besides Connors and I left alive in this melee.

I hurdled the corpse and kept on. The Kiwais were now setting the hut afire from outside. I found one of them in my sights and raked him with automatic fire, hitting him in the arm, neck and back. He jerked about like a rag doll on a string, and then hit the dirt on his own torch, his body now burning in the flame. I ran around to the other side of the building, and found the other Kiwai setting a fire at the only entrance of the place. Again I banged out a message with the Sten, and he was slammed against the hut wall, then dumped unceremoniously in a sitting position, his bloody guts hanging down onto his hip.

The fire was now raging at the building, and there were screams coming from inside. I started through the flames to the interior, but the heat was too intense. If I did not do something fast, the women and children inside would roast alive.

I turned and saw Connors nearby, heading toward me. *"Get some people over here with water!"* I yelled. *"All you can find!"*

Connors nodded, and turned to get help. I kicked sand onto the fire from the ground, but it was too well established for that kind of assault. There was more screaming, and a Bamu woman came running out through the flames, coughing and yelling. Her lap-lap had caught fire as she emerged, and now she was burning. I threw her to the ground and rolled her over once, smothering the flames, and burning my hands in the process.

"Stay inside!" I yelled, not knowing if they could hear or understand, or if the advice was sound.

I turned to head toward the other big hut, and a Kiwai raced toward me with a rifle, his eyes wild. I blasted at him with the Sten, and he did a sidewise flip, hitting the ground hard on his side. Racing to the other hut, I opened the door-flap and yelled that we needed help.

Women soon came streaming from the hut, and with some warriors Connors got to help, we put the fire out and the building and its occupants were saved. The women came choking out of the interior, some burned, some holding children. A few of them had been asphyxiated before they could get out, and one of those was the Kiwai girl who had felt it necessary to entertain me, earlier, in that same hut.

While the fire was being brought under control, with the black smoke mixing with the bitter odor of gunpowder, suddenly Kokoda called his people back.

I was surprised, because I had thought we were not holding at all. But apparently he felt the need to re-group, and as quickly as the attack had begun, it was over. Kiwais were retreating back to their positions across the clearing and in the jungle, and the sound of gunfire trickled down to sporadic bursts, and then quit.

I went to the barricades and looked across the clearing, and could see Kokoda over there, looking clean and regal in his bright feathers, very much in command and control.

The clearing between us and them was literally littered with bodies, just as it had been on Kandam Plain. Very few were Bamus out there, but there were plenty of them behind the barriers. They lay all around me like cordwood, in all kinds of positions that the human body only assumes in death. There were beheaded corpses, and others that had been mutilated badly. As at Kandam, many of the dead had been riddled with bullets so savagely that they were bloody messes. That was another thing I could not seem to control—the wasting of ammunition by pumping one enemy warrior full of lead, before turning to kill another one. It was the most unusual war with guns that I had ever been in.

Now the Kiwais were back re-forming, and the fighting was over for the moment. A Bamu woman came up to me on her own, thanking me for saving the women and children in the hut, and then suddenly Connors limped up, with bandages for my hands.

We sat down in the shade of the undamaged big hut, as Merah strode along the barriers, re-grouping our defenders. Connors wrapped my hands with gauze to keep dirt out of the superficial burns, and we did not talk at all until he was finished. Then he looked into my face somberly. His cheek was dirt-smeared, and he looked very ragged.

"Well," he said.

"Yeah," I muttered.

"They really got to us, didn't they?"

"They gave us a lot of casualties," I replied. Where Merah walked along the barriers, there were only a third of the warriors we had had before the Kiwai attack. "Why did he leave off? Why didn't Kokoda wipe us out?"

"He couldn't see how bad off we were," Connors offered. "He'll be getting his reports now. He'll be back, all right. Sooner than we want to see him. How do you estimate our chances?"

I looked over at Connors. In a way, I had gotten him into this, almost as much as Burke Ardrey. He had been very lucky to survive the first attack, considering his inability to move around well.

"They're lousy, Connors," I told him.

He nodded. "That's the way I see it, old sport."

"Most of our ammo is gone. And a lot of our people that are left are wounded. The mortars, grenades—even the Stens—won't play a part in the next attack. I'm going to concentrate my fire against the frontal rush this time, and we're going to have to get across to our people that once they've downed an enemy, they must forget him and go on to killing other Kiwais."

Connors licked dry lips. "Is there any way out, Rainey?" he said slowly, asking the inevitable question. "Can't we try a withdrawal of some kind?"

I held his sober gaze with mine. "I don't want to lie to you, Major. Kokoda has men behind us in numbers. I got a good look during the attack. No, we couldn't break out of here. And there's no way to slip away, either, for us. Not in broad daylight. It looks like our only choice is to fight."

As I uttered those words, a slow chanting began across the clearing in the Kiwai ranks, and this time it seemed particularly ominous and blood-chilling.

Connors looked toward the sound. "What you're saying, old man, is that we're bloody likely never to leave this place."

I glanced over toward our barriers, and saw Merah's warriors, bloody and dirt-streaked, hauling corpses away so there would be room to fight again; when that chanting stopped. Merah and every one of his Bamus already knew the answer to Connors' suggestion to me.

"I'd have to consider that the most likely possibility," I said heavily.

TWELVE

"Issue each man twenty rounds of ammunition," I told our last Kikori trooper, as he and I strode along behind the barriers together. "When that's gone, the fight will be pretty much over."

"Yes, sir," he replied stiffly. He was the only man left from the force Connors and I had brought with us. He was wounded but still ambulatory.

"I want them lined up behind these barricades in two lines," I continued, feeling the heat of the boiling sun on me under the Aussie hat. I had to talk above the chanting of the Kiwais, only a short distance away. "That way we can mass our firepower. Nobody should fire until he can hit something. I'll give a signal for the first firing."

"I understand, Major Rainey," the private said.

It was bizarre. We were going through the motions of a real defense, when we all knew now that there was none. But it was pointless to think of what was going to happen when Kokoda sent those masses of armed Kiwais at us again. It was pointless to talk of death and finality.

The chanting of our enemy was louder now, and Kokoda had placed his spearmen out in his front ranks, with their decorated shields and gaudy war-paint. They danced out there now, in unison, as the chanting rose in pitch behind them, and I stared across that hot, dusty field and wished I had just one .50 caliber machine gun, even now. It could make the difference. Even having ammo for the Stens would have given us a chance of sorts. But it was gone. And so was most hope for survival.

Our Bamus were a ragged-looking lot now. Their wounded bodies sagged behind the barriers, and their painted faces revealed their private encounters with the reality of the coming massacre.

The Kiwais, though, smelled an easy victory now, and were working themselves up to a fever pitch. I got a glimpse of Kokoda over there, striding arrogantly behind his lines, and wondered if he would be strutting in the streets of Kikori one day soon. And then Port Moresby.

Kokoda had proved himself a worthy opponent. Most tribal chiefs would not have come back for such punishment after Kandam, numbers or no numbers. He had shown great leadership qualities, and I thought it too bad that they had not been able to civilize him in Bik Pella. It was going to take strong men like Kokoda to bring these savages out of the jungle some day. But not with guns, to kill every white man and native who had a different idea from Kokoda's.

I looked around for Merah, and did not see him. He had looked very despondent when the first attack was finished, and I thought he was not as strong a man without Zigibi. That was often the case with primitive leaders—they depended on subordinates, particularly religious and medicine men, more than they liked to admit. I went up to the partially-burned community hut, where Connors sat on a make-shift chair in the shade. He had a pencil and paper on his lap, and was staring out across the village blankly. His ruddy face was tired-looking and lined with fatigue. He was not the same man who had come out there to show Kokoda what was what. Neither was I. I went and leaned against the hut beside him.

"Writing a letter home?" I joked, trying to relieve the tension. "You may have a little trouble with delivery."

Connors tried a grin, but it was not very successful. "It's a will, actually."

My face settled into straight lines. Somehow I did not feel like cracking any jokes about that. "A reasonable precaution," I said, "in these circumstances. I should probably have one, myself. The trouble is, there's no one left back in Texas to leave anything to. And the other trouble is, there isn't all that much to leave."

Connors grunted. "There's this girl back in Canberra. Lovely little thing. You'd like her, Rainey. I met her on my first furlough back there, and she's been there waiting every other time I've gone back. Dru, her name is. Silly little wench. I told her last trip to get married, but she says she's waiting for me. To get transferred back, you see. Bloody crazy little wench."

Connors stared out across the compound, and Kokoda's warriors made their racket in the background. We figured there would be no second attack until all of that stopped. It was quiet between us for a few minutes, as Connors remembered some private things. Finally, I spoke.

"And it's the girl that's getting your estate?"

Connors nodded. "There isn't much, Rainey. A small bank account in Kikori. And a plot of ground outside Canberra, in rolling hills. I wanted to farm it some day."

"Soldiers can't count on retirement, it seems," I offered. "But who knows, Connors? Maybe you'll see the farm yet."

"Maybe the Sepik delta will become a Port Moresby garden overnight," Connors said wryly. He gave the piece of paper to me. "Have I said enough, Rainey? You know more about these bloody things than me."

I took the will and read it aloud. "*'I, Averill Connors, being of sound mind and spirit despite these unpleasant circumstances, do hereby make this last will in anticipation of my impending demise, at the hands of the Kiwai tribe and Motu Kokoda, who are planning an advance into our fortified position at a site called by us Bamu Village One. My entire estate is to be given over to my friend and companion Drucilla Riley of Canberra, upon evidence by the Army that my life has been forfeit in the service of my country and for the advancement of reason among the savages of New Guinea. God save the Queen.'*"

I sighed deeply, and looked up at Connors. He was watching my face, eager to be told that he had done what he hoped to, in the writing. Thinking more of that than his own possible death.

"I couldn't have said it better myself," I told him. "What are you going to do with it?"

He took the paper back. "I hadn't thought. I suppose it would be unsafe on my person. Maybe I'll put it in the big hut. Where it might be found by someone coming through here to find out what happened to us."

"Merah might be able to find a hiding place for you," I told him. I looked at the ground. "Connors, you're in lousy shape to fight. I'm going to be frank with you, I don't see how you can help much when this starts up again. I'd like to hide you along with your will."

Connors squinted at me. "What?"

"I thought maybe we'd dig a hole inside one of the small huts, big enough for you to lie in, and cover it good, to make it look like the dirt floor of the hut. Maybe it would work. Maybe Kokoda would think you had gotten past his lines, in the fighting. If you survived, we would have someone to maybe get back to Kikori and tell them what happened here."

Connors was looking at me as if I were insane. "Good God, Rainey! What in the bloody hell do you think I am, man? Does a soldier hide in a bloody hole when the fighting starts? What the bleeding devil did I come out here for?"

I had had no idea Connors would be so outraged by the suggestion. I just saw no point in his laying down his life without being able to fight back much. "You're a good soldier, Major. But you should be in a hospital, not on the battlefield. Look at your bandage. Your side wound is bleeding again. And you have only one arm to use. You can't heft a carbine that way. All you'll have is the few shells left in your revolver."

"That will be enough to take a couple of Kiwais with me before they put me down," Connors said tightly. "No, I couldn't hide out while the rest of you were being slaughtered, Rainey. This is more my war than yours. I'll see it through."

I nodded gravely. "I understand," I told him. "I'd be the same way, if it were me." I slapped him lightly on the shoulder. "I'm going to go find Merah. It's about time he gave his people a little pep talk, I think. It won't be long before Kokoda's warriors come again."

"I don't know if you'll get much out of him," Connors told me. "He looked rather down, I'd say, when I saw him last. He headed toward the—"

Connors was suddenly interrupted by a muffled explosion, from the direction of the unburned community hut, where Merah had gone not long before. Some bamboo was blown off the side of the structure, and white smoke wafted out through the new aperture.

"What the hell—" I muttered.

"Merah is in there!" Connors exlaimed.

We both rushed to the doorway of the hut. I drew the Star .45 at my hip and pulled the door-flap back and went in. Connors came in after me.

When I got inside in the dim light there, I had to squint to see. But it did not take long to discover Merah. He lay on the dirt floor, across the hut, on his back.

Connors and I exchanged glances, and Connors mumbled an obscenity under his breath. We walked over to Merah, and I knelt beside him.

It was all pretty bloody. Merah had kept a grenade out from the supplies, apparently, and had chosen to commit suicide by holding the weapon to his stomach. He did not want to be around when Kokoda came for his head.

The grenade had ruptured his middle belly. Blood and flesh were all over the dirt floor around him, and he was almost cut in half by the explosion. Oddly, he was still very much alive. His left hand lay in the mess that was his mid-section, covered with crimson, and his eyes were open and staring up at us.

"For Christ's sake, Merah," I said bitterly.

"The bloody fool," Connors added.

Merah worked his jaw. "Merah—make-walk to —Great River," he grated out, almost inaudibly. "Kokoda get—too-empty—head."

He was cheating Kokoda of taking his head from him alive. But the selfish bastard might be robbing us of our thousand-to-one shot of putting up a reasonable fight against the Kiwais. Without Merah behind Connors and me, it was a different situation. When the Bamus found out their leader had given up already, it would be tough as hell to get them to put up any resistance against Kokoda and his raucous headhunters.

Merah moved his mouth again. "Kokoda not—" He trailed off at that point, and a thin worm of crimson appeared at the corner of his mouth, and his eyes glazed over.

Merah was dead.

I rose from beside him. "Maybe we can keep this from the others," I said heavily. "If we don't let anybody in here—"

We turned at a sound behind us. It was two Bamu warriors with carbines, and they were staring hard at Merah from behind their red and yellow war paint.

"Oh, Christ," Connors said grimly.

Within five minutes, most of our people had left the barricades to gather around the outside of the big hut. They looked scared now—much more so than before. They no longer wanted to fight. Bamus fought to protect their leaders and their leader had left this world.

"*Get back to your positions!*" Connors shouted at them. "*The Kiwais will be here at any minute!*" He was saying it in Bamu and I was not getting every word, but I figured out the meaning.

None of them left the hut area. The barricades were deserted, and the Kiwais were at a fever pitch, chanting and shouting across the clearing.

I strode along their ranks, looking into their dark, wild faces. "Translate for me, please, Major," I said to Connors.

Connors nodded.

"*Kokoda is ready to come again,*" I said loudly to them. "*He wants your heads for his trophy poles.*"

There was no response from them, when Connors repeated it.

"*Do you want to hand yourselves over to him like cattle at a stockyard?*" I said. "*Is that the way the great Bamu warriors meet a challenge?*"

A warrior stepped forward a pace, still clutching his carbine. He made a short speech in Bamu, and then Connors turned to me. "The fellow says Merah has set them an example. Merah did not fight this last fight, so they don't know why they should."

I tried to keep the impatience and anger out of my voice. I held my hands up for all to see the bandages. "*I helped save your women from Kiwai torches. Do you think I did that for Merah? There is such a thing as personal honor. The gods watch each of you apart from your chief and your priest.*

They do not want to see Bamu warriors give up to Kokoda without a fight. They hope you will show your individual greatness today, and your Bamu courage, in making Kokoda pay dearly for any Bamu head he takes."

Connors translated, and they listened carefully. As he spoke, I saw some dark faces change. Finally Connors was finished.

"Now return to your positions," I told them. *"Return and fight for Bamu glory!"*

Not one moved at first, after Connors' brief translation. But then one rather tall warrior turned and headed for the barricades, and another followed. In a moment, they were all turning and going back to their positions, one by one, and silently. When Connors and I were alone again, he turned to me.

"You did it, Rainey. You got our thousand-to-one shot back, old boy. And our chance to die like soldiers."

I made a face. "Not my highest ambition in life, I'm afraid. But better than letting Kokoda come in here and—"

I stopped, and listened. There was a sudden silence in the jungle that was almost like a noise. The Kiwais had stopped their thunderous chanting, and were suddenly deathly quiet. They were ready. Not a bird called out around us, nor was there any other jungle sound. The stone-age world around us had stopped on its axis for a brief moment in eternity, waiting.

"It looks as if Kokoda is coming," Connors said, with his suddenly dry mouth and flushed face.

We went to the barriers and looked across at

the lines of Kiwais. They looked almost as many as before. There was one thin line of spearmen, and then all those Volkssturm rifles were massed behind them. Kokoda came out to their fore, and raised his arm toward me.

"We come now for the great Rainey!"

Connors and I exchanged glances. "That's quite an honor, lad," Connors half-grinned.

I shook my head slowly, then turned and let Kokoda see me. *"Come and do your worst, Kokoda!"*

Some of my people turned and looked toward me, then a clamor slowly rose among them, and in a moment a great shouting and yelling was going on. It was answered by the Kiwais. I turned and strode along behind the Bamus.

"You in the front. On your knees, and rest the carbines on something if you can. Don't fire until I give the signal, and then make every shot count." Connors came along behind me, repeating in Bamu. "You people in the second file, keep your standing position until a man goes down in front of you, then take his place. But you'll fire with the others, so they'll get a double dose. When your ammo is gone, there won't be any more. Use the rifle as a club, but keep killing Kiwais."

Connors translated rapidly, and when he was finished, a loud hue and cry came from the Kiwais, and Kokoda had given the signal for their attack.

They came faster and more wildly than in the first attack. The Kiwai spearmen came running like demons toward our lines, with the riflemen in several waves behind them, and their yelling as they came was spine-chilling. My people did not fire a shot until I gave the signal, after the spearmen were right on us and leaping the barriers and their riflemen were already firing into us. Then I dropped my arm and Connors yelled the command in Bamu, and there was a thunderous volley from our ranks.

The devastating effect of our fire on the Kiwais was impressive to watch. They went down in big numbers, all along the line, and then those behind the fallen ones went down. In moments no voice could be heard above the clattering gunfire, and the smoke was so thick you could not see through it. The Kiwai spearmen were either down or were behind our lines, and we paid little further attention to them. But the women swarmed from the big hut and surrounded the spearmen like locusts, hacking at them with knives and machetes, apparently worked up by my speech to the warriors, and grateful to me for helping save them from the fire.

The riflemen of Kokoda kept coming in big waves, and we kept firing back. Our people were beginning to go down, too, but we were taking a lot of Kiwais with us. I had never seen a more brutal encounter of two forces with guns. It was a stand-up, slug-it-out firefight of violent savagery, with both sides fighting to keep their heads on their shoulders.

"Keep firing!" I was screaming at them. *"Keep killing the enemy!"*

"Take their rifles when yours is empty!" Connors yelled. I saw him throw his carbine down, and grab up a Volkssturm that had just fallen at his feet, when a Kiwai who had leapt the barrier had fallen dead near him.

Kokoda had held a heavy wave of riflemen back, and they were waiting for his signal to come roaring into our ranks now. I jumped the barricade in that momentary lull and began grabbing up VK-98's and throwing them over the barriers to my people who had run out of ammo. *"Here! Take these and use them!"* I yelled.

There were Kiwais all around me, firing into our ranks. When they spotted me out there, a few of them began trying to pick me off. Slugs whizzed past my head and tugged at my tunic, but I got very lucky and was not hit. I kept grabbing the guns and heaving them over the barriers, taking them from Kiwai corpses that were riddled with gunfire. The top of one warrior's head had been blown off neatly, as if done by a surgical instrument. I pulled a rifle from his death grip. Another one had had his entire face blown away when the slug hit him, and I had to pry his gun from under his torso. I now piled guns in my arms, and was trying to shoot back occasionally with my Star .45.

"Rainey! Get to hell back here, you bloody fool!" I heard Connors' voice come to me, from behind the barricades.

But our people needed firepower, and I was getting them some. I stepped over Kiwai corpses to get at another gun that was within easy reach. I glanced and saw Kokoda over there, staring hard at me as if I must be crazy. I guess I was, a little. All I could think of was giving our people a last chance to put up a decent fight.

Then Kokoda yelled something in Kiwai, and I heard my name, and they began yelling and running at us again, and I knew Kokoda had given them specific orders to get me. I turned and strode to the barrier and dumped the rifles there, and my people grabbed them and began using them against the new onslaught. Without bothering to go behind the barriers again, I turned to meet the new attack. I knew we could not last through it, anyway. Our people were down to a handful. The Kiwais came yelling and screaming, and our people fired their last heavy volleys and knocked a lot of them down. I stood out there in the open, angry with myself for leading the Bamus into this slaughter, firing the Star into the charging Kiwais and hitting one with every shot.

"Come on, damn you, you devils!" I yelled. *"Come and get my head if you can!"*

I cannot explain the next few minutes in that battle. The Kiwai shells were flying all around me, and not one connected. I kept firing the Star, and then jammed another magazine into the gun and shot. They were piling up in a circle around me, and I seemed unkillable for those moments. A spearman ran up very close to me then, as if reverting to primitive weaponry might negate my magic, and heaved the weapon at my chest. But I twisted slightly and it merely ripped my tunic, putting a shallow gash in my side beneath it. I shot him in the face and he did a backwards somersault and hit the dirt.

The Kiwai riflemen in that charge had slowed down and stalled now, not just because of our last withering fire, but apparently because of my presence out there beyond the barricades. But I knew that when Kokoda urged them onward, we would fold before their attack now like paper cut-out soldiers. We were finished.

"*Come on back, Rainey!*" I could hear Connors' feeble plea, from behind me.

But I knew that it made little difference now whether I died behind the barrier or out in front of it. I raised the Star above my head. "*What's the matter, don't you know when you've beaten us? Don't you want to fill your trophy poles?*" I was taunting them, because I wanted it to be over with. "*Come on and eat our lead, damn you!*"

Kokoda was standing out in the open over there, too, and he was staring at me strangely, as if he had never seen a white man act quite like this before. Then he did something that amazed and confused me completely. He raised his arm and yelled something in Kiwai, and his warriors began falling back to their original positions.

I stared unbelieving as the Kiwais fell back, and the shooting gradually stopped between our groups. Our people had only a few rounds left, anyway. Kokoda called his warriors back into the long lines, leaving the body-littered field empty of live troops.

Connors came up behind me and leaned on the barricade. "What the hell is he doing, Rainey?"

I squinted across the field in the boiling sun, sweat running down my face. I had lost the Aussie hat, and my hair was down across my forehead. The Star hung in my right hand, its barrel still hot. "I'll be damned if I know," I muttered. "I guess he knows he's got us, and wants to give us time to think about our heads decorating his poles."

But in the next few minutes, the most unusual

things happened that I had seen in all the wars I had fought in around the world. Kokoda lined up his most colorful spearmen that we had not killed, in his front ranks, with their long shields and deadly-looking spears and weirdly-painted faces, and then he shouted out a long, piercing chant in Kiwai. The chant was then echoed by the entire rank and file of Kiwai warriors, and the spearmen shook the long shields in time with the staccato words. Kokoda repeated the sing-song chant, and again the warriors boomed the echo of it across the clearing, waving the shields toward us.

"What the hell is all that?" I said aloud.

Connors came over the barrier, limping, to me, and his face had an odd look in it. *"By Jesus! I don't believe it, Rainey!"* he said harshly.

I looked at him as he came up beside me.

"Kokoda is saluting you," Connors said slowly and numbly. "The bloody bastard is saluting your military genius!"

I turned back toward Kokoda and his Kiwai. Kokoda gave the chant again, and it was roared across the clearing by his people. Then the spearmen parted and the ranks of riflemen came forward, to the center of the clearing, looking very grim, forming ranks there with their VK-98's.

"A last honor before the big kill?" I wondered aloud.

But I was wrong. Kokoda came up in front of his warriors, and looked at me long and solemnly, and then gave a command. To my astonishment, they stooped and laid down the rifles in the tall grass, where the corpses of their comrades lay rotting in the sun.

"Bloody hell!" Connors muttered.

"I'll be damned," I said.

They had voluntarily disarmed themselves.

Kokoda now came forward from his troops. I stuffed the Star into its holster, and walked out and met him in that fly-buzzing, bloody field. When we met out there, we just stared into each other's faces for a long moment.

"You will not kill the last of your enemies, Kokoda?" I asked him out there in the sun.

He shook his head. "You are the greatest white man I have ever met, Rainey," he said solemnly. "A brilliant strategist and a brave soldier. I regret that you are not Kiwai. But you have made your point to me. To kill a brave enemy accomplishes nothing. You and Major Connors are welcome to come to my territory at any time, to talk peace and how the Kiwai may eventually be represented in the bik pella government."

With those words, and without waiting for a reply from me, Kokoda turned and walked away. His warriors broke ranks then, and followed him into the jungle across the clearing. One by one the Bamus behind me rose to watch the departure, dumbfounded. In just a few minutes, the Kiwai were gone.

I turned and walked back to Connors. "You heard him?" I said.

"I heard," he said hollowly. "It's absolutely incredible, Rainey. You're probably the first white man who ever held Kokoda's respect. So he gave you our lives as a tribute to you. You'll be a bloody jungle legend out here, by Jesus."

I grunted in my throat. "I just wonder if any of that will help me get rid of this strange physical sensation that's just come over me."

Connors glanced at the fresh crimson on my tunic. "Are you all right?"

I suppressed a grin. "Uh-huh. Except for the presence of this suddenly weighty object still attached securely to my shoulders—my head."

Connors stared at me blankly for a moment, then a laugh began deep in his chest, and came bursting forth not unlike the staccato gunfire that had so recently filled the morning with its clamor. I found myself joining him, and our laughter echoed over the clearing and through the primeval jungle around us, and our surviving Bamus looked at us as if we had suddenly gone as crazy as Kokoda.

That did not bother us, though. I knew, as I helped Connors back into the village, that we had done what we came out there for, and more. We had freed that bush country from the terror of modern arms, and all that they stood for.

And we had given back to Kokoda, and to all these inhabitants of this forest wilderness, a gift more important than his to us.

We had given them their future.